T0266637

THE HAUNTED SCREEN

THE
HAUNTED
SCREEN

J. M. TYREE

DEEP
VELLUM

Dallas, Texas

A
STRANGE
OBJECT

Austin, Texas

Published by A Strange Object, an imprint of Deep Vellum

Deep Vellum is a 501(c)(3) nonprofit literary arts organization founded in 2013 with the mission to bring the world into conversation through literature.

Copyright © 2024 J. M. Tyree. All rights reserved.

No part of this book may be used or reproduced in any manner without written permission from the publisher, except in the context of reviews.

Library of Congress Cataloging-in-Publication Data

Names: Tyree, J. M. (Joshua M.), author.
Title: The haunted screen / J.M. Tyree.
Description: Dallas, Texas : Deep Vellum/A Strange Object, 2024.
Identifiers: LCCN 2024022787 (print) | LCCN 2024022788 (ebook) |
    ISBN 9781646053490 (trade paperback) | ISBN 9781646053612
    (ebook)
Subjects: LCGFT: Thrillers (Fiction) | Novellas.
Classification: LCC PS3620.Y753 H38 2024 (print) | LCC PS3620.Y753
    (ebook) | DDC 813/.6--dc23/eng/20240517
LC record available at https://lccn.loc.gov/2024022787
LC ebook record available at https://lccn.loc.gov/2024022788

Cover design by Emily Mahon
Interior design and layout by Amber Morena

Printed in Canada

Todt ist die Erde . . .
The Earth is dead . . .
—HÖLDERLIN

THE HAUNTED SCREEN

ONE

We moved for my wife's summer academic teaching appointment to a central European country with deep philosophical traditions, centuries of musical genius, a complicated language that retained the dative case, earth-shattering beer, fun pastries, gruesome fairy tales, and hideous scars and stains on its modern history. I think you know the country I mean.

My wife, Rebecca, is Jewish and biracial. Her parents refused to visit us while we were in Germany. Rebecca's father, born in Montserrat, grew up in a London suburb with a wartime airbase that was hit by Nazi bombers and

V-2 rockets, one of which reduced a neighbor friend's house to rubble and claimed the life of the kid's mother. Rebecca's mother's people were from outside Kraków. They'd emigrated to New Jersey when Rebecca was thirteen, leaving her linguistically and culturally all over the map.

Rebecca's curiosity about everything German made a certain peculiar sense in light of all this, and the feeling was instantly mutual. She taught her courses on Anglo-Caribbean Postcolonial Literature in the ancient university town in the forest on the river with the multicolored gingerbread medieval houses from vacation snapshots of the world's most famous colleges. The university faculty's idea of dying and going to heaven was having a ridiculously attractive Jewish professor with brown skin lecturing on C. L. R. James's books on cricket. ("My father was a Black spin-bowler from Hornchurch who married a tough Jewish Jersey girl," her first lecture began, to a rapping of knuckles on desks.) Rebecca found that she didn't mind the experience of being exoticized, at least as a temporary novelty, since the enthusiasm struck her as genuinely intellectual and the Germans seemed to know considerably more about Communism in the Antilles than many of her white American colleagues back at her home institution, a small liberal arts college in Vermont. I felt differently. Some of the attention they lavished on her talks seemed nice enough, some of it felt weird and over-bearing, some of it felt like an apology of some kind or another, some of it was clearly motivated by abject lust, and some of it induced mild paranoia about everything unspeakable lying under the surface of the most placid place on the planet.

We were housed in a modern apartment block on the hills overlooking the town, adjacent to fields, horse farms, and a nature reserve with paths for solitary walkers, singing groups of picnicking students, and sun-leathered old couples addicted to body culture who hobbled along vast miles with the aid of Scandinavian metal walking sticks that looked like ski poles. The old-fashioned among them occasionally blurted out a *"Grüß Gott!"* or a *"Hallo,"* but the convention was not to greet strangers. Maybe the person you encountered was contemplating their thesis on Hegel or was a latter-day Hölderlin—the philosopher had passed through this area, and the poet had gone mad living in this town, wandering these hills and writing po-ems about the river and the trees.

I was supposed to take this time to complete my own book, a study of Hitchcock's *Vertigo* based on my PhD dissertation. Having no appointments or projects of my own—besides basic shopping tasks and house-husbandry—and quickly realizing that the bus ride into town gave me severe motion sickness on the winding roads down the hills, I spent a lot of my time walking alone, deep in the forest. I also felt I was walking into the past. Into the deserted woodcutters' roads, the recently cut trees spray-painted with the names of the places where the wood was going to be shipped. Through cathedral pines and mossy birches, along a stream that led to an ancient monastery, which always seemed to be closing when I arrived in the late afternoon. Or to the beer garden overlooking the vast rolling hills, popular as a way station with hikers, bicyclists, and families. Under peach and magenta-flecked clouds at moody twilight, the hills rippled away towards the south, beyond which lay Lake Constance and Switzerland. (Hölderlin had walked across the border for a tutoring job, and, if I recalled correctly, had crossed the lake by rowboat. The poet was always tramping long distances—as far away as France—on failed quests for meager teaching work. He had fallen in love, I had read, with the mother of one of his students, causing a career-wrecking scandal.)

Another trail led along the ridge out of town, passing a picture-postcard village with a church spire nestled into the valley below, just a few kilometers from the modern university hospital research facilities. These jaunts of-

ten took place when Rebecca was having drinks down
in town with new colleagues. I was always invited but
I sensed that she needed some autonomy, and my German was execrable, so I pleaded motion sickness and set
off by myself.

I was also walking into my personal past, on a memory quest for an old lover. Amy had been my unstable
charismatic professor in graduate school in New York.
She had liberally abused her power over me on many
long nights as well as recommending me to her editor
at the fancy publisher that had accepted my half-baked
book proposal on *Vertigo*, swayed by Amy's assertion that
I would produce a crossover title on the production history of the so-called greatest film of all time. I was drawn
to Amy's radioactive core of negativity and the sense that
she might spontaneously combust with intellectual fire at
any moment in one of her lectures. With Amy's promised
preface and her seal of approval, the book sold almost
overnight in a wildly implausible sequence of events. The
fact that the book did not exist only increased its appeal,
I sensed, for the editor, who also had been a former student of Amy's.

But the truth was that my research was not advanced
enough to be groundbreaking and my writing was not
fluent enough to appeal to general audiences. I would

need to hire a ghostwriter. When I pointed out these concerns to Amy, she offered to cowrite "our book" without credit, which only served to undermine my confidence further.

While I was her student, Amy had spent her sabbatical year here in this same German town, studying Expressionist horror films from the 1920s. We had exchanged searing, embarrassing letters on delicate blue vintage airmail paper while I was finishing up my dissertation. Things went downhill on my research soon after she lost interest in my body.

Rebecca didn't know very much about Amy or that Amy was my secret reason for my long walks in the German woods. Amy had described this forest to me in such detail that I felt I had been here before. She had also described happenings in the forest that she could not explain, things she'd seen that had disturbed her, and which I had assumed at the time were either metaphors of her inner mental state (always tangled and at times unhinged) or else fictions she had spun for my delectation. Amy had mentioned leaving notes for others to find in various locations in the woods, and I made it my personal mission to see if I could find some of them while I was here. I had brought our old correspondence with me, trying to find clues in the text for the locations that might match up with real places in the trees.

But her writing was sometimes difficult to follow, and her descriptions included lines like, *I fucked your dream-face again in the moss of the birch at the end of a galaxy of poppies.* Amy and I had lost touch—okay, she ghosted me—but I planned to write to her and see what she remembered of this place. It might please her to hear from me, I thought, in my sick pathetic way, hating myself for the thought and then lapping up phrases from her letters, angry black ink in all caps marking indentations and sometimes tears and rips in the soft blankets of folded blue paper. I licked at pools of what looked like squid ink dried in the margins like little dark orgasmic blooms and placed my ear on Amy's description of my "lovely neck," cribbed from *Nosferatu.*

On these walks I was often in a state of tainted solitude, visiting two places and times at once, remembering how nobody asked about the little bruises left by Amy's fingertips above my collarbone at my dissertation defense, at which I thought it would be sophisticated to wear a V-neck sweater that displayed her handiwork. Besides Rebecca and the surly employees of the discount grocery store on the hill, who genuinely relished their contempt for foreigners for breaking shopping and bagging protocols unknown to them, I did not have anyone to talk to in this country. I barely spoke two hundred words of the language, knew nothing of the territory where I was living, and might have just as easily disappeared without anyone noticing.

Even Rebecca might not have minded very much, at least that was my fear. In her demeanor and body language, from the beginning she had clearly conveyed an unspoken wish to have a frolic, away or apart from me. It wasn't a cruel or unreasonable attitude. She wasn't indifferent. She just wanted a vacation from us, or from my depression and uncool uselessness as a trailing spouse, my failure to finish my *Vertigo* book despite the annual drop of concerned emails that had morphed into threats to rescind my advance. I should have stayed back at our home in Vermont, as she had suggested before our departure. Now, she offered to pay my way home. It sounded strange to think this way, but I had stayed on more for Amy than anything else. I was afraid to ask Rebecca to slap me.

On my walks, I stopped carrying my mobile phone with me. I hadn't bothered to find an adapter cord, and I was worried about international roaming charges. This experience reminded me what life was like before The Glow of omnipresent screens, during the first half of my life, way back in the twentieth century. Everything around me felt doubly new, since I was exploring without a map and had nothing to record, reflect, mirror, crop, or preserve what I was seeing. This was a kind of magic trick or time-traveling illusion that impacted my cortical tissue and gave me a dozen encounters an hour with trees and birds that I burned to share, deep down in a splendid clear reservoir of loneliness. The building complex had around a dozen categories of recycling bins but no Wi-Fi. After turning off my phone, I stopped answering emails, then lost touch with the news. The world outside the forest faded. And given the state of the world, this isolation had its points. I got thinner and fitter and my head started to look sleek, slightly snakelike, and oddly German, with my sleepy blue eyes and graying blond hair. If I wore gray socks, brown shoes, a shirt with a collar, and a wool sweater, I could pass, visually.

On these walks, my head also flooded with memories from my childhood, growing up in a Midwestern town as a latchkey kid with a single mom who often had to work until seven or eight at night, leaving me to spend my after-school hours by myself in the local library until it closed, listening to *Alfred Hitchcock Presents* horror stories on a turntable with giant headphones while I watched the LP turn at 33 rpm. Hitchcock had trained as a filmmaker in Germany. Another LP in the library stack contained German lessons, I recalled. I had chosen unwisely in not pursuing the language, but my mother was Czech and hated everything German about our beery, blond, cow-infested, sports-crazed, schnapps-heavy corner of Wisconsin. I remembered that I had always held hands with horror. Those Hitchcoctions of murders and ghosts comforted me because they encompassed the worst that could happen—impossibly, supernaturally bad things— but then, unlike in real life, the story ended, and the vinyl record went back into its snug case. Darkness fell and I moped home in my discount sneakers to the meals of spaghetti and chili replete with ground round that my exhausted mother managed to conjure for me before collapsing in front of PBS.

Gradually it dawned on me during my forest walks that something was terribly wrong with the nightmare perfection of the entire area. You would catch a whiff of something deep and rotten when you visited the university campus and saw placards with images of Nazi gatherings on the tranquil island in the river. From that spot, you could also see the castle on the hill, where the local museum housed some of humankind's earliest and oldest figurines, sculptures, and musical instruments—horses, bears, fertility goddesses, and flutes carved from mammoth ivory by the cave dwellers who lived in the hills nearby, tens of thousands of years ago. The spot where the NSDAP rallies took place also had a view of the tower in which Hölderlin lived after he went mad. He had been saved from the city asylum by a carpenter who had enjoyed reading his novel, proof, if needed, that a good book only requires a single sympathetic reader. The asylum had been state of the art for its day, meaning that the innovative techniques for treating mental illness and severe depression involved immersing the patients in cages filled with near-freezing water.

You must make a friend of horror. The phrase, ad-libbed by a problematic star from a vanished era of cinema classics, came from a Vietnam war movie, but it was true anywhere and Germany was the place where Brando's words became inescapable to me.

Anyway, it was out there in the dreaming woods outside Tübingen near dusk that I began to develop the sensation that I was being watched or followed. Maybe it was a lack of decent sleep, or my depression, or a worsening of my eye condition, misshapen corneas which required specialized contact lenses to correct, but I began to glimpse small, odd shapes and briefly illuminated sparks drifting at the edge of my vision. Sounds of distant voices or nearby breathing seemed to emanate from the forest. Amy had described something similar in her letters, so maybe her hallucinations had transferred to me somehow. These could have been students kissing in the woods, littering the wildflowers with their sighs. Or the sounds might have been caused by resting pilgrims making their way on the thousand-mile trek from here to Santiago de Compostela—the monastery in the woods was on one of the ancient walking paths that wound through sacred sites in Germany, Switzerland, France, and Spain.

But no, something else was happening, either in the woods or in my head. The little sparkles and the sighing noises started to join, and I had the sensation that someone or something occasionally brushed my neck. It felt cold and dry, not like human fingers but like the wings of a moth or a midge. I could never find physical evidence that I had been touched. And I wasn't certain that the bright designs I saw or the animal noises I heard were connected. Or real. Wild boar roamed these forests, Amy had claimed in her letters. It might have been birds in the brush, or foxes (were there foxes here?). It could have been a brain tumor playing tricks, or my family history finally asserting itself. I couldn't rule out my hope that I was imagining most of it. Surely it is possible to make yourself see things, in a certain mood, at dusk, in the shadow of toxic love, or the impending darkness of fairy tales, fever visions, and evil history that haunted this land. The old trees read my mind and turned the contents of my brain inside out. Something dark had affixed itself to me, an extra weight.

TWO

Mental illness swam in my DNA, lurking and waiting to be activated. When I started to see and hear things in the woods that probably weren't there, I couldn't help thinking about my mother's psychotic break, back home in suburban Milwaukee, that little pocket of Teutonic madness that lies hidden and dormant inside Middle America. It happened when I was in college. I had gone to visit my mom during the summer break and found her unwashed, down below a hundred pounds. She was terrified of taking a shower. She claimed that the water smelled sour and had been polluted or poisoned somehow. She confided that someone was living in a secret cupboard hidden in the paneling of her bathroom's wall. This figure was tall and very thin and would emerge at night to point an impossibly long finger at her—it knew secrets from the past and cataloged the worst things my mom had done.

"Your life is a lie," the figure would say. It also screamed out abuse and obscenities, calling down ethnic slurs on my mother's head.

My mom had fostered Stevie, a teenager originally from Haiti, for the year after I'd left for college, to refill the nest. Stevie had disappeared one day and, a few months later, had been found dead from an overdose of opioids. My mom blamed herself because the entry-level pills had been pilfered from her cabinet.

"This house is white!" the figure shrieked, according to my mother, adding that it had used a word banned in our family. "I decree that you are no longer white! You have to *earn* it, bitch."

None of those modern corporate antipsychotics had done anything to help my mom. She had been in and out of various wards and hospitals in the area for "suicidal ideation."

Her illness started to ease as soon as she had been ingesting lithium for a few months. The change was gradual but drastic and positive. It was as if her brain was an ocean sponge that had dried out or had been denied the right balance of saline. Like the tissue had grown brittle and starved of some vital nutrient or mineral. The cortex crumbled in on itself, misfiring and generating demons. The lithium appeared to work like bath salts you could sprinkle into the brain fluid, easing it back into the nourishing water. It massaged its way into the deep tissue and calmed the confusion of mixed-up neurotransmitters that had been mistranslated into phantoms and terrors. My mother's brain slowly became resilient again. The lithium brought her back from the verge of death.

Before the lithium was prescribed, I had spent the worst month of my life as her caregiver. I wasn't sure she was going to make it. I waged a relentless campaign, every hour of every day, trying to persuade her to take a shower and eat enough to stay alive.

"Why won't you eat?" I would ask her, four times a day.

"I can't stand the smell," she said, but the food was fine.

"Why are you afraid of the bath?"

"The water stinks," she said. "They recycle it, you know. It's sewage."

At the time, it felt to me like she had been cursed or possessed. A medieval worldview began to assert itself. Personality was a spirit that inhabited you and might drift off elsewhere or be replaced by another presence that did not mean well. Later, I recognized these movie cliches as products of my own fear and inability to accept her illness. What all of it was, was suffering, and watching a person you loved suffering.

My mom came back from the abyss, but things were weird. She seemed to have changed in odd ways I found difficult to understand. I returned from college for a long weekend break, and we ate at Perkins restaurant. My mom now wanted me to call her Grace, which was not her name, but which represented, she explained, a force or personage that had saved her life. She ate new dishes she had never liked before, most especially the bottomless pots of drip coffee and the desserts that Perkins made their specialty, Black Forest cake and lemon curd pie. She rapidly gained back all of her lost weight and then began adding pounds, which delighted me. Her jokes became very ghoulish and dry. Seeing an ambulance with flashing lights parked at the restaurant one evening, she said, "I guess a table is opening up."

I learned to live with my mom and Grace, but I never felt that she was herself again. It was much better than losing her altogether.

Out in the woods of Germany, so many years later, I turned over my mom's case in my mind as I walked in the woods searching for the places Amy had described in her letters and wondered when I would succumb completely to the nervous breakdown I feared I might be having. I had forbidden myself to contact Amy, although I thought it might be a good idea to reach out, if only to finish the book, so that it might be closed, rather than so heavily bookmarked, unfinished, staring back at me from the shelf. If only out of professional courtesy, to request that Amy complete her preface to my work and confirm that she remained willing to support my work. Pretending that I was spending my days on research, I didn't have the heart to tell Rebecca—or anyone else—that there was no book.

In my early thirties I'd met Rebecca at an academic conference and I had never been completely honest with her about the way that Amy had taken advantage of our situation to milk me for sex when I was younger. It wasn't something I felt like I could refuse and remain in her orbit. Physically, my body responded without my consent. I discovered that I liked getting hit, but I wanted to be asked first, rather than asking. Rebecca had a self-righteous ethical compass about professional standards, and she might have put word out in the academic community about Amy if she found out about her abuse of power. She also might have told me to rescind my publication offer and return my book advance.

The problem in my book was one of translation. My

dissertation was all academic-y and heavy-duty film theory. The publisher had been promised a rollicking thrill ride, a title that would captivate both students and librarians with the secret inner workings of the production of Hitchcock's greatest movie. Nothing of the kind existed in my computer files. But I found out that nobody really cared. The editor who had acquired the book had left publishing for business school. The contract remained active, but the new editor never replied to my emails after I explained that I needed another year or two.

I needed Amy's help, and not just about the book, which seemed increasingly silly and remote, nothing more than a pretext for getting back in touch. I needed to ask her about what had happened to her here, in this place, that had made her hallucinate in the forest. I spent an entire morning composing an email in my notebook, tearing out the pages after each draft and ripping them up into smaller and smaller pieces. When I had something that seemed less desperate and needy, I braved my motion sickness, took the bus into town, and found the world's last remaining internet café. The person running the desk was South Asian and dressed up as Super Mario. They wore their red-rimmed heart-shaped sunglasses indoors. They stood up and moved towards the door when I entered, pressing a clanking Zippo lighter at the tip of a clove cigarette.

"Wow," they said when they saw me, in English.

"Wow?" I said.

They removed their dark glasses and I saw that their pupils pinning within their liquid brown irises.

"Yeah, wow," they said. "Feel that?"

Their accent was neither German nor English nor American.

"What?" I said.

"All these dark shapes passing through our bodies? Like dozens of tiny earthquakes?"

Maybe something weird had gotten into the water supply down here, I thought.

"I just need to send an email," I said.

"Do you, though?" they said. "Do you, really? Do any of us *need* to send an email?"

They started to push past me so that the smoke wouldn't cover the room, with its recesses of outdated desktops and clear plastic dividers between them covered in stickers for satanic-sounding pretentious metal bands.

"How much is it?" I asked.

They looked me over, inhaling and blowing the clove-infused smoke out into the daylight from the half-open door.

"Twelve euro?" they said.

"For an email?"

"For an hour. It's a one-hour minimum. You can browse

for white tube socks or Stinger missiles. Point being, all your searches here are anonymous, with our signature logless VPN."

They gestured me over to a terminal next to a rail-thin young woman with a pageboy haircut, a Crime and the City Solution T-shirt, and a Fidelio-style costume mask on the other side of the divider, whispering angrily through white plastic earbuds.

"*Nein!*" she said in a very loud whisper. Then she shouted very loudly while slamming her fist against the table. "*Nein! Nein! Nein! Nein! Nein!*"

I peered around the divider, out of instinct, just to see if she was okay. But the woman wasn't speaking to anyone, she was recording a video. Now I was in the background of her video.

"What are you looking at?" she yelled at me in English.

"Sorry to disturb you," I said.

"No, this is perfect," she said. "I'm rehearsing for a casting call. Video's still running. I'm keeping this in. Official welcome from the Channel to our imperial American overlords!"

Disoriented by this encounter, I exited frame and tried to mind my own business in the makeshift cubicle adjacent. I quickly typed my handwritten message into an email, listening to the whoosh from my inbox as my words winged across continents, my heart in my throat.

Amy had an auto-reply on that seemed specific to my email. It read as follows: *What's happening to you is what happened to me. That's because time folds and dreamers are connected in their dreams. I'll see you in mine and you'll see me in yours. I will haunt you and you will end up like me. We exchanged our diseases. I'm M and you are W. I've traveled inside Krampf's camera. This is our story, and the ending is the one you fear the most. What you are seeing there is what I am seeing here. There's a little gray shape following me through the streets. It wants to kill me. It's saying that my death will look more like a suicide than an accident, but it will be a murder. Does it kind of sparkle? Can you hear it breathing in the woods? Is it getting closer? Pay close attention. I'm watching. I will join you soon, my darling with the lovely neck.*

I churned out a few alarmed pleas for an explanation, but nothing came back except the same auto-response.

"*I am going to burn down the world,*" the young woman sang in a convincing low growl on her side of the plastic divider. "*I am going to tear down everything.* Today on the Channel it's still 1991. We meet the girl and plant the bomb with Radio Werewolf's *Songs for the End of the World* and Lars von Trier's werewolf movie, *Europa*."

Did Amy know where I was? She had not specified any location in particular in her auto-reply. While I was waiting around to see if she would respond, I decided to stalk myself online to see what I could see. First

I searched for my own name. It didn't take long to connect me with Rebecca, and then to discover that Rebecca had been awarded a prestigious sabbatical in Tübingen. If Amy had dug around for half an hour—she could have surmised my current location without any aid from the ethereal realm. In the paranoid-sounding state conveyed by her message, it might have seemed to her like more than a coincidence that I was in the place where she had been all those years ago when we were pen pals and when she was having visual and auditory hallucinations. Put two and two together in that condition and it added up to seven.

Clearly Amy had started connecting a web of invisible dots into a cat's cradle of manic threads. But that explanation only went so far. I really was seeing things and hearing things out in the woods. How Amy seemed to know what was happening to me, I couldn't explain, yet. It freaked me out. I closed my email window. My last message to Amy had been something along the lines of "I hope you're okay."

As I stood up to leave, the young woman gestured for me to move closer and enter into the frame of her video again.

"How long can you hold your breath?" she said.

"Sorry?" I said.

"Want to find out?" she said. "How long you can hold your breath?"

"Were you even born in the twentieth century?" I said. "Why 1991? Do you know 'Planet of Sound'?"

"Do you know *The Oath of Black Blood*?" she said.

On my way out, Super Mario told me I was welcome back any time to use the rest of my prepaid twenty-seven minutes of connectivity.

"Can I donate those minutes to her?" I asked, gesturing at the masked woman at the computer. "Is she okay?"

"She's teetering."

"Aren't we all," I said.

"She'll be all right as long she stays within the postpunk orbit," Super Mario said.

"She mentioned something about an oath," I said. "Black blood?"

"Too bad. I get worried when they start talking about how they belong in the woods."

"Why?" I asked. "What's going on out there?"

Super Mario shrugged.

THREE

On the bus ride back to our flat, dizziness forced me to get out and walk before I reached my destination. Bright lights popped at the edge of my vision, and I started to unravel.

"Ich hasse Schwindelgefühl," I tried to explain to the driver regarding my quick exit, and getting the basic verb wrong, mistakenly saying that I hated vertigo rather than that I had vertigo.

"Hasse?"

He looked offended, thinking that I hated his driving or that I was implying that his driving made me sick.

"Habe."

A torrent of German sentences and gestures followed me out of the bus, but I was too ill to follow whether he was cursing me or offering advice for medical attention.

Vertigo is an uncanny experience because it can be induced simply by thinking about it, or by watching a movie of a car traveling on mountain roads, or even through the action of memory alone. I can remember, with perfect clarity—every sound and smell—all the places where I've gotten sick.

I remember a town square in Costa Rica in the hills outside of San Jose where my soul almost left my body through my guts. I was only there for an hour, and I had never been there before, or returned since. I do not recall the name of the town, but part of me is trapped there forever. Rich green-smelling air, some of the cleanest air on the planet, lush rainforest air, distant mist in palms, ochre earth that looked edible lining the cliffside roads where I came to grief and split myself in two again and again in an effort not to vomit inside the coach. A person with kind eyes who was selling powdered tamarind at a kiosk observed a helpless American lose his bile and give up on living, and they interceded, asking if I needed water.

Vertigo—the derangement of the bird-mind's inner

compass—never stops once it has begun. You can use it to time travel via wormholes in alternate dimensions. If you have it bad, you can repeat the experience with virtually identical effect just by thinking yourself backwards. It wouldn't be an exaggeration to suggest that vertigo is the opposite of the feeling of love. It's a kind of living death when you can feel it creeping up on you and you know there is nothing that will stop it.

One of the awful aspects of its spiraling logic is the sinking, sickening impression that the whole thing is all in your mind and surely could be stopped with more self-control. The brain turns against itself, the inner ear controls all sense of time, everything slows to a near halt, the past becomes present, and all the other times the sickness happened before start to recur, helping to hasten the vertigo along, assisting in the building waves of nausea. It's as if the mind were being drilled like a tree—drilled for a core sample across its rings. In fact, motion sickness, at its most severe, could drive its sufferers to welcome a trepanning through the skull, if someone said it would relieve the agony.

I sat on a park bench in the placid suburbs and waited for the world and its dark blotches and shimmering flares to settle into a more acceptable and established order. I was near the entrance to a museum of contemporary art,

ten minutes' walk from our flat, although it might as well
have been five miles. The art museum was festooned with
placards advertising a lecture series on psychoanalysis
and film. I thought of Amy and her descent into her personal abyss. She had been working on a hotly anticipated,
long-delayed book of film history based on a reconsider-
ation of Expressionism and horror cinema in 1920s Germany that was being compared, long before publication,
with Lotte Eisner's *The Haunted Screen* and Siegfried Kra-
cauer's *From Caligari to Hitler*. But I had read some of her
manuscript and notes and had found the prose difficult
to untangle. Telling her as much was the cause of the initial breach in our friendship. A lot of her project had to
do with the secret societies and occult groups that partly
funded German film productions like *Nosferatu* and ad-
hered to alchemical fantasies about film's supposedly
supernatural powers to preserve time and affix images
of the dead to a living continuum that would outlive the
physical dissolution of the body. Some of the film's producers had believed such things, but now it seemed that
Amy did, too. A thread emerged in her manuscript about
a bridge between worlds or parallel worlds connected by
a dark shape in the forests that F. W. Murnau supposedly
had captured with cinematographer Günther Krampf's
camera. The film was then defaced or altered afterwards

for reasons that Amy claimed to have uncovered in an archive of previously unpublished letters written in a terrified state of mind by Murnau to his screenwriter, Henrik Galeen.

Amy had refused to share her research images of the Murnau letters, claiming they were cursed and would corrode my life if I read them in full. According to Amy, Galeen reported other disturbing incidents during the filming of the second version *The Student of Prague* with Krampf several years after *Nosferatu*. Some of the rushes had captured unscripted figures appearing in a mirror despite not being visible to anyone on set during the day of shooting. The footage, once again, had been destroyed or possibly hidden in a location that Galeen refused to disclose. Something had gotten into Krampf's camera, or something about the camera had been able to make unseen things visible, words to that effect. Krampf later worked in Britain with Hitchcock on two lesser-known French-language wartime propaganda pictures, which is how, Amy theorized, Hitchcock might have found out about the strange camera.

Some old enemies in Amy's scholarly circles claimed she had forged the Murnau-Galeen letters, or had them forged, or that they didn't actually exist, due to her secrecy and unwillingness to provide proof. I wasn't so sure. Amy was clearly going through something, but she was the smartest person I'd ever met. Since then, Amy's publisher had dropped her book. Her status as a star of film criticism had been questioned and her reputation as "the next Sontag"—a critic who got her picture on the *front* cover of her books—had been scaled back. Rumors of personal outbursts at colleagues had swirled along with accusations of misconduct with younger scholar boys like myself, although I never would have complained about the chance to sleep with her.

So far none of this had stopped Amy from producing research at a tremendous (even slightly alarming) rate, although she had shifted away from books and regularly aired out her conspiracy theories online, where free-speech crusaders allowed her to write, revise, alter, and expand her lengthy, widely shared posts, in the process developing a cult following and sowing confusion among students who quoted and cited her "controversial" articles in their undergraduate papers, to the despair of their professors. Her new reputation as a quasi-celebrity hot-prof-gone-bad wasn't hurt by the prominent inclusion of author photographs featuring a blond wig, extraordinarily expensive designer sunglasses, and a super-high-end green leather jacket that emphasized certain curves.

Because of the "suppression" of Amy's research by "institutional elites" (as she described it), Amy had cashed in on her cancellation. She regularly appeared on various far-right podcasts whose producers and hosts relished her suave toxicity as well as her intellectual street cred, not to mention the dodgy connections to Crowley and the German occult in the life of *Nosferatu's* producer, Albin Grau. Amy happily reprised her theory that Grau and Murnau had really discovered something on location, and that there was evidence of it in certain shapes and shadows left in the film. According to Amy, remnants of these images persisted in one scene in which a negative image is spliced directly into the film. This was done to hide something. The scene occurred at the point when the film's protagonist, Thomas Hutter, played by Gustav von Wangenheim, crosses over into what the intertitles call "the land of shadows," after entering the carriage of the vampire on the way to his castle. Based on certain landmarks in the image, Amy claimed that the scenes were shot in the forests near Tübingen, not in the other locations near Nosferatu's castle that other scholars had long assumed to be the film locations.

Thinking of Amy in my own bedraggled state, I felt like I was hanging from a building over an abyss, grasping at a flimsy drainpipe, watching the structure to which I was clinging start to bend and crumple from my weight, looking down into the canyon between buildings where I would fall, the ground seeming to rush forwards towards me already, no visible means of escape. The film to which I had dedicated my stalled academic career was often read as a dream because the protagonist, Scottie, played by Jimmy Stewart, starts out the movie in a situation from which rescue is impossible. There was an old theory that, for this reason, the entire story of *Vertigo*—absurd and implausible—was a fantasy or flight of fancy, a story concocted entirely in the mind of Scottie while he hung from the building and waited to fall and die.

This helped to explain why nothing that happened in *Vertigo* felt real. *Vertigo* meant ridiculous plot twists, nonsensical character motivations, inexplicably self-destructive acts. Amy knew that I suffered from motion sickness, but that was a superficial, surface-level reason to send me into *Vertigo*'s spirals. It was the relentlessly pathological idea of love that fascinated both of us most about the film, and which she encouraged me to study in great depth, as if there were some answer to a mystery about *her* embedded somewhere in the story of the film's production. She speculated that Krampf's cursed or magical camera had made its way to California in Hitchcock's hands. The idea of me and my research as a kind of sequel to her and hers—and *Vertigo* as a continuation of the occult mysteries of the German films Hitchcock had studied during his apprentice years directing his first films in and around Munich—turned her on. She floated the idea of publishing her notes on *Vertigo* under my name.

"Mad love, self-destruction, repetition compulsion, unclean," Amy told me once, without a trace of self-consciousness, soon after she'd noticed me in her lectures, on my first visit to her house as her newly minted research assistant, after hours, after wine, after putting Galeen's version of *The Student of Prague*, that classic German silent film about doubles and mirrors, on the DVD player. Soon I realized that I had fallen into a trap that I didn't understand how to exit without losing a limb, or my academic fellowship.

"When you lose yourself, where do you go?" she said. "Your tongue had better be supple. Get to work, my lovely man."

She demanded that I strangle her and that she strangle me in order to multiply the power of our orgasms, but my heart wasn't in it and she could tell. So she sighed and rolled over me, powering through in the saddle, bucking and levitating, trying to make it hurt. I couldn't come that way, I was too scared, though Amy enjoyed it more that way, because it lasted. When she came, she bit me so hard that my chest turned yellow and purple the next

day, with the image of her incisors embedded in my skin
for a week. I was stupidly proud of these badges at first.

I remembered those first encounters with Amy while
I staggered back through the nice neighborhoods that
lined the ridges of the streets leading up to the university housing on the hill adjacent to the fields and the forests above the obscenely picturesque town where Murnau and Krampf supposedly had filmed something that
frightened them and, long before that, where Hölderlin
had been tortured with hydrotherapy because he was
seeing things and hearing voices out in the woods. It
wasn't God, his doctors insisted, it wasn't angels or demons or anything very interesting at all. Just humdrum
you, the mind boiling itself alive.

FOUR

Rebecca and I had been assigned to a ground-floor flat with a patio that led out to a public footpath winding between the concrete high-rises that jutted improbably out of the corner of the woods. These tower blocks overlooking the town and the mountains beyond provided housing for foreign faculty and visiting scholars from across the globe. I knew there was something wrong with my mental state because these horrible buildings enthralled me, whereas I could find no joy in the wonders of the ancient university and its cozy environs down in the valley along the splendid river, with its joyous singing students crowding their drunken boats all summer long. I seemed to have lost the taste for life or even a basic sense of what was beautiful and what was not. The massed blond youth made me feel a little bit sick—it wasn't their fault, they didn't know what was about to hit them, and in a way they were brave to be enjoying life at all in the face of impending darkness all around, as the lamps went out one by one across Europe and America.

Old Germany, nice Germany, premodern postcard Germany, on the other hand, left me feeling creeped out. The charming street market faced the town hall and the magnificent ancient clock that chimed above the cobbled square. Crowds gathered from all over the world to drink Aperol spritzes and listen to a brass band oompah their way through classical standards. There was a plaque near a window denoting the place where Jewish families hid during the roundups. Every timber and wattle building splashed with cheery colors was a portal into the nightmare.

Walking back to our flat from the bus stop after my head cleared a little, I came across two broken-looking men near our building who had set up a game of pétanque, using the gravel of the parking lot in place of a lawn for their bowling game. I took a seat in the grass nearby and watched them set up their games again and again.

This was the simplest fun imaginable—fling steel balls as close as possible to the target jack, knock the other players' ball away, or try to hit the jack itself closer to your balls or farther from your opponents'. The players never once acknowledged my existence, but their lack of interest in me as a spectator brought me an odd comfort, and my motion sickness eased off further. I imagined that these two men might be old friends who had played thousands of rounds together without getting bored with the game or with each other. Because of their ravaged faces, I pictured the pair playing this game in unpaved lots in North Africa or in refugee camps in Greece after a rough crossing with people smugglers, stages along the way to Germany during the million-person migration.

I had forgotten how to have a friend, a most embarrassing and most American disease. What was I doing here?

"Do you see me?" I asked them as I stood up to go, and they did not even flick their eyes in my direction. Maybe I had not spoken loudly enough, or maybe they were not pleased to be addressed in English or maybe they had learned something bitter about Americans in their journeys or maybe they were used to people with nothing positive to say.

I remembered how catatonic Jimmy Stewart gets as Scottie in *Vertigo* after he's convinced he's seen the woman he loves throw herself off a church tower. The loss of love breaks his spirit. He's so shocked and horrified, the film has us believe, that he fails to look at the face of the corpse, which cannot be identical with the face he loves, since that is Judy Barton, and the dead woman is Madeleine Elster. As viewers, we never see Madeleine's face. The plot involves an absurdly elaborate ruse in which Judy has conspired with Gavin Elster, Madeleine's husband, to murder Madeleine under circumstances that Scottie will mistake for suicide at the church tower. But Judy falls in love with Scottie and that love will lead to the unraveling of the murder plot as well as to her own doom, and Scottie's. The movie was all wrong. It needed to be retold, Amy had always said, at least several times, from the perspectives of the women in the movie, first from Judy's point of view, then from Madeleine's. Hitchcock had made the wrong film or had failed to complete the story. Midge, Scottie's friend, ex-fiancée, and self-appointed "mother," must have her say. The mysterious nun whose appearance at the end of the film drives Judy to jump from the bell tower should also be heard. What was her story?

Watching the pétanque players calmed me down enough to return to our flat. What I found there drove my blood pressure back up immediately and filled my head with rotating loops of anxiety and paranoia.

Our door hung open to the corridor. Rebecca wasn't home. Nothing inside the flat had been touched, but a new item had appeared. It was a large brown paper envelope, manuscript-sized. My name was on the package, but it didn't have an address or any stamps. So it had been hand-delivered during a break-in. When I opened it up, I found typed pages inside. It was the draft of a book called *Further Mysteries of the Haunted Screen*. The author, according to the first page, was me.

I flipped through the first few pages. The manuscript was dedicated to an "M," reminding me of Amy's strange auto-reply email message, in which she had claimed that letter for herself and assigned me a "W," as though we were inverted images of one another. The book began with this nonsense: *Where to start? Why this movie of all movies? What is it about* Vertigo *that makes us all return and rewatch, again and again? This is a personal journey through a film considered to be among the greatest of all time, on every Top 10 list. The film is a love-object and a death-trap. Once you watch the film, you spend the rest of your life inside it. The director's evil spell draws on a deeper well of secret knowledge acquired during his years training as a filmmaker in 1920s Germany, and Hitchcock's encounters with a cursed silent film camera that reveals the world as it really is, not as it appears to our eyes. The camera reveals the truth about the nightmares surrounding us everywhere. Clues embedded in Hitchcock's film reveal the precise location of this cursed camera, which, no matter where it is pointed, reveals what is happening in real time in a wooded spot near Tübingen, Germany. Bilocation to Tübingen is possible from other sites of power revealed by the camera.*

I was distracted from the pages by my impending fear that Amy was so easily able to invade my privacy. Had she been here herself in our apartment, and, if so, what else had she done—or what other things had she hidden away—while she was here? Or maybe she hired someone from the local area to deliver this package in a way that would frighten me. Her mind was completely dissolving, from the sound of the manuscript. What had she said about some presence that had attached itself to her? If Amy was stalking me, or had paid someone else to stalk me, it was bad enough. It couldn't be true, what she had claimed about the camera and the things in the forest.

I decided not to tell Rebecca what was happening until I could clarify things. I didn't want her to panic, I told myself. Or was it that I didn't want her to send me away? That was the logical thing for me to do—decamp back to our place in Vermont. In a small corner of my mind and my heart, Amy had taken up residence again. If she was here, she clearly needed help, and she might listen to me if I could find her.

I drew the curtains and sat down with Amy's manuscript on *Vertigo*, riffling through the pages at random
to see whether there were any clues. I found a section in
which she wrote about the comments of one of Hitchcock's biographers about his use of Jimmy Stewart and
Cary Grant as his male leads. The result was a double
vision of the filmmaker's self-image. Whenever you see
Grant onscreen, she summarized the biographer, you're
seeing Hitchcock as he wished he was—swashbuck-
ling, resourceful, brassy, confident, and suave, masterful
around women, whatever Grant's real-life proclivities.
When you see Stewart, on the other hand, you're seeing
Hitchcock as he always feared he was. Weak, voyeuris-
tic, nervous, passive, and helpless. Take Scottie's catatonic
depression after he witnesses the death of Madeleine in
her fall from the tower, thinking that he has failed to pre-
vent her suicide. The suicide, in turn, has been brought
on by Madeleine's apparent possession by the dead spirit
of Carlotta Valdes. Amy wrote (or had inscribed in my
voice) that nobody ever considered the possibility that
Madeleine had somehow outlived her death and had possessed Judy. Secret methods, she continued, might exist
for bilocation and passing into another person's body by
means of image projection in parallel dimensions.

I remembered that Amy's auto-reply claimed she was
being pursued to the death by some sort of supernat-

ural force. We were both in danger, according to her. I understood this as a metaphor, but I didn't entirely discount what she was saying. I did seem to be suffering from something that was causing me to hallucinate. It did feel like joy had been stripped out of the world. My libido had ebbed away, much to Rebecca's disgruntlement. The throngs of tourists in their summer clothes down in town, searching for frivolities and distractions, so eager to exchange glances with anyone they mistook for a local, German blonds and sophisticated-looking women with blockish glasses, colorful scarves, and henna in their hair, the bare legs of summer, the global women's fashion craze for yoga pants, the pageantry of display in all of its harmless flirtatiousness and fun—all of it lodged in my brain but failed to register any normal level of wonder, curiosity, or even basic lust. All this transient fun— Rebecca's world of riverside beer gardens, lithe younger people in paddleboats spilling out over the surface of the river, couples holding hands on the park benches, university drinks soirees—all of it made me want to cry, except that I couldn't even cry.

Amy's words, on the other hand, weird as they were, quickened my heart. They called me down into the vortex of the past, marked with memories of sex in which she had hit me out of the blue with her open palm, scratched my flanks with her nails, or pulled me down to her by my hair. Once she had smacked me with a block of wood that had fallen off the frame of the bed as we were fucking, leaving a rectangular mark on my bruised ribs. I reacted with fright, trying to jump up to flee, but she held me down, and I let her. In other moods Amy said she loved to suck my cock, but this was just amped-up talk out of dirty films. Maybe it would be more accurate to say that she liked to watch me react, taking pleasure in the knowledge that she could really hurt me if she wanted to, not that I minded, although it would have been nicer if she asked me first. Her look, scleral language directed at me from above or below, said, *See? Now you know what you are.*

These were things that didn't interest Rebecca very much, although she certainly wasn't prim. She lived for little luxuries like eating black licorice in bed and calf rubs after soft-landing her closed-eye orgasms. I told myself I preferred this, too, and I did, for her, but not for me. But I didn't know how to ask for what I really wanted, shaming myself into thinking it was wrong, and I didn't know how to articulate that I wanted to agree to being smacked around before it actually happened.

I still fantasized about Amy's dark aggression because it made me feel alive, or, rather, reanimated. I was an undead soul, wandering, invisible. I belonged to her even

now. I needed to go back into the woods—to be alone
with whatever was haunting us. I went out in the evening light when everything looked tinged with an under-
sea atmosphere. I took the path into the nature park along
the allotments and sheds that overlooked the town and
the river and the mountains in their blue distance. Girls
on horseback were clomping through the paths, calmly
wending home to stables in the hills, oblivious to the dis-
tresses of middle age, and showing no evidence of noticing anything sinister in the forest whatsoever. They
were strong and friendly girls, and they anchored me in
the knowledge that whatever was happening to me was
a problem for adults whose souls were already dead or
badly damaged. The forest was just a forest. The trees
were trees. Birds gleaned in the thickets and the hedges
before night fell, the orchards stretched into the sunset,
and the fading sunlight revealed everything harmless in
the world to best effect. No sparkles pursued me at the
edge of my vision.

Then I passed by an electricity box with some graffiti on it reading MDEAD in black spray paint. The letters were disarranged so that the "M" floated. An upside-
down cross was sprayed to the left of the jumble. It was
a band name, maybe, some gothy tag of a local street art-

ist who had wandered up here from campus. Once I saw this sign, I could not seem to walk any farther. It was like a warning seal that repelled me from the path. MDEAD became M. DEAD. Amy was here, somehow, watching and listening, waiting for me somewhere deeper in the forest, sending signals through nine time zones, through the past, through a little army of graffiti couriers and metalheads, disciples or ghosts in this town who were eager to do her bidding. The horse girls had long passed me by, and I was alone at dusk waiting to be confronted by some dark force. The spots and blotches and bright sparks drifting across my field of vision began to return, attaching themselves to sounds in the trees and flitting shapes that disappeared when I turned to confront them.

I would make a doctor's appointment in the morning.

Despite the late hour, Rebecca wasn't home by the time I made my way back to our flat, in the darkness below the first planets and stars. She did not return that night. I stayed up and read Amy's book, trying to determine if there were any clues in it. I couldn't sleep. It wasn't just Rebecca's absence or Amy's tangled lines and brainwaves. There was a child screaming for hours somewhere in our building. The sound seemed to be coming from just below or adjacent to our bedroom. It was the sound of pure torture that only kids, with their utter lack of emotional proportion, can make when they feel distress. It must have been a family new to the building and maybe the screaming child had jet lag. It sounded like a tender person being lowered into a vat of boiling oil.

FIVE

I charged up my phone and brought it with me to my doctor's appointment, rightly assuming that I could connect to Wi-Fi there while I was waiting in the clinic. Amy had received my messages from the internet café and replied with an invitation to chat. A green light appeared next to her profile in my contacts list, indicating her availability. I clicked on her and immediately felt a confused rush.

You got my message, Amy wrote as soon as she saw that I was logged in.

What time is it where you are? I wrote.

No reply.

What's MDEAD? I wrote.

No reply.

Someone broke in, I wrote. *I read your book.*

I'm being followed too, she wrote.

By who?

By what is more the question.

And why? I added.

No reply.

Once again she described a dark shape that sometimes appeared in the corner of her eye, like a little cloud that dispersed into tiny droplets as soon as she turned to face it and scattered on sight.

I'm not allowed to see it fully yet, she wrote.

This dark shape had affixed itself to her window, she wrote, where she had moved into an apartment near the Mission Dolores, soon after she had looked through the camera she claimed had supernatural capacities, given to Hitchcock by Krampf and now located in a private archive in the Bay Area she refused to name. Her place was near the church from *Vertigo* where the graveyard held the tombstone of Carlotta Valdes. Judy, playing Madeleine for Scottie, drew him to the spot during one of her wandering episodes, her fugue states, where she crisscrossed the city and visited sites connected with Carlotta, giving Scottie the impression that the dead woman's soul had possessed hers. Amy thought her proximity to Carlotta's grave would help her write, but it had turned out another way.

It wants us both dead, she wrote.

I assumed Amy was referring to the gray shape, and I decided to take a risk.

I've seen it, too, I wrote.

This has to be connected to those woods, she replied. *You have to help me find out what's happening. It knows that we're connected. We're experiencing the same things thousands of miles apart. Or maybe I'm closer than you think. Notice anything different around you?*

Where are you? I wrote.

I can be there with you in the woods any time I want, she wrote.

Amy exerted her magnetism on me even through the keyboard and the screen, as if our fingers were touching when we typed together. I remembered how she looked like she wanted to stab me to death after a shower, plump shoulders and muscular legs, still holding her razor, grinning under a dyed green buzz cut before she fastened on a red or blond wig, upper lip slightly turned toward her nose, lower lip slightly bee-stung and swollen from kissing herself roughly in the mirror-steam. I liked to watch her reading film theory in bed with her *Garden of Earthly*

Delights Bosch bookmark from the Prado in a scholarly volume by Miriam Hansen on German critics from the 1920s.

In dreams, Amy typed, *the gray shape sometimes takes on the dimensions of an oblong box and I am buried inside of it with your severed head. Did I slice you open yet? Or is that supposed to happen in the future? I can't remember.*

I ignored the more violent comments—Amy being Amy. During night walks in the city of *Vertigo,* she continued, she would sometimes sense something shifting after her in the darkness as she neared home and the Mission Dolores. The thing sort of flung itself out of view by the time she turned to face it.

I didn't say anything, but Amy's messages were beginning to make me feel better, not worse. Something was slightly amiss in her story. I had been to the Mission Dolores, many years ago, and of course I knew that there was no real Carlotta Valdes buried there. The grave was created just for the movie. It wasn't possible that this fictional burial place of a fictional character had any relationship with what was happening to Amy in reality.

I also realized, reading Amy's messages, that my own account would sound similar when I rehearsed them for the doctor. What was happening to me was slightly different, and less extreme, than what Amy was experiencing. She felt herself to be under full supernatural attack. I wanted to help Amy, but I also recognized that at least some of my own hallucinations might be chalked up to the power of suggestion. Yes, a delusion, I thought, how comforting.

Thanks for the book, I wrote. *I don't know why you won't publish it under your own name.*

Can't you feel it, she replied. *You know it's for real.*

What does your mind doctor say? I wrote back.

She thinks everything is a metaphor.

Of what? For what?

My book, Amy wrote. *Your book.*

I can't take credit for your work.

The ellipses danced in the chat window, indicating that Amy was still typing.

She couldn't climax easily anymore, she had told me during our affair, because of her antidepressants. That's why she tried out more extreme scenarios during sex. One night I had broken through this problem in the opposite way. I set my phone's timer for twenty minutes and focused entirely on licking the letters M and W into her pussy. The idea had come from a psychotherapist's advice about orgasms, which was to eliminate all goal-oriented thinking and focus exclusively on play. She came and then said it was bullshit, never do that again.

I think this fucker can fly, Amy continued writing about the dark shape. *When it's following me, it senses that I'm about to turn around and it kind of dissolves upwards into the air. Is this what's happening to you?*

Not as bad, I wrote.

There's something evil out there, she wrote.

I laughed a little bit to myself, reading those words. It wasn't the idea but the words that sounded silly. I had to admit that the more messages we exchanged, the better I felt. Listening to my own delusions being described by someone else, I realized how ridiculous they sounded. Or maybe it was simply the thrill of being in contact with Amy again, or the comfort of recognition. Someone who knew what being undead felt like.

How did you get your book into my house? I said.

I walked through the fog, Amy wrote.

What's "MDEAD"?

The ellipses danced for a while, but no words materialized from the cloud. It was as though Amy was typing and then deleting what she'd typed before pressing the button to send the message. She didn't reply to that question but instead started another train of thought.

Not sure I should tell you this, Amy wrote. *You're living right near where I first saw it. It followed me out here from those woods.*

Tell me how it happened. That might help.

I was in the little museum in the castle. Have you been there?

Sure.

So you know that collection of figurines?

Amy was talking about the university's collection of Ice Age miniature sculptures. They were some of the oldest works of art created anywhere in Europe, probably around 40,000 years ago, in the caves near Ulm, just down the river. The figures featured chubby goddesses, bears, geese, and delicate horses' heads carved from mastodon ivory. An array of primitive flutes—among the first surviving musical instruments made by human hands, according to the placards—lay under glass while hidden speakers piped in whistling sounds that demonstrated what these flutes might have sounded like.

So did you see the Lion-person there? Amy wrote.

I'm not sure.

It's a shape-shifter, with the head of a lion and the body of a man.

Oh, is that what's following you around?

Something was in the woods, she wrote. *There were all kinds of predatory creatures in the hills back then. There is something wrong with some of the trees in those woods.*

What do you mean?

They don't look right, some of them. It's like they have shapes embedded in them. Like the trees have . . . I don't know . . . captured something inside of their trunks. Bear trees. Snake trunks.

Hmmm . . . I typed, smiling to myself. My lips curled around my front teeth in unselfconscious skepticism. Dark shapes, animal-people, tree-creatures.

Amy wrote about encountering one tree in particular, on a walk deeper into the forest. She described a tree that looked like a tree but was not a tree. Reading that broke the spell entirely. I had had enough. I couldn't tell over the chat interface whether Amy really believed what she was saying or whether she was throwing spaghetti at the wall to see what would stick. Maybe she had made up everything, including her dark shape. Whatever she was doing, even if she didn't know what she was doing, it wasn't nice. Amy wasn't nice. That was her attraction and her repulsion. I was supposed to believe that our depressions were linked to a supernatural force out in the woods. It was absurd and manipulative, and I felt that I had fallen for something akin to hypnosis.

When the psychiatrist emerged into the waiting room at the Uni-Kliniken, I put down my phone like a child caught doing something bad in school. The doctor was one of those suave fiftysomething guys with a shaved head who had the gaunt sunburnt face and oddly thin neck of a compulsive runner. He'd agreed to see me on short notice, he explained, because he thought I'd told the staff at the front desk that I'd sustained a brain injury. When I had tried to describe my condition in German, I said that something was wrong with my head, but maybe I'd failed to use the correct subvocabulary.

"It's inside my head," I tried explaining at first in German, then in English.

"How do you know this?" the doctor asked, and we were off to the epistemological races in our mistranslations. "Are you in the military?"

Perhaps he was trying to screen me for signs of violent derangement.

"I'm unemployed," I said, trying to stick with my weak German, so that I was speaking in German and the doctor was replying, seamlessly, in English. "My wife teaches here at the university. I am a person who is bad, living in a shitworld. What is inside me, inside my head, is shit."

"Let's switch over to English," he said. "Tell me your story. I've got five minutes, and you are interesting."

He brought me into a small but immaculate examination room. I gave him a précis of almost everything that had happened—hallucinating in the woods, old lover contacting me to claim our lives were in danger, apartment broken into. Amy's theory of an evil presence living in the middle of the tranquil ancient forest above the town.

"But this is not correct," the doctor chided me. "This is not in your head. We have witches locally. You must see a witch."

"Sorry?"

"Some say," he started, and then, thought better of this approach, suppressing a slight smile. "Some of the little villages hereabouts—hereabouts?"

"The idiom would be 'around here,' I think."

"Some of the villages around here have a festival," he continued, "dedicated to our witches. They dress up as animals and so on. You have seen wolf-people, lion-people, yes? Probably they are practicing in the Naturpark and playing with your mind. There is no cause for concern. These are ancient folkloric traditions with contemporary botanical medical applications."

"This is more like a dark shape at the edge of my vision," I said. "Which kind of sparkles."

"Witchkind of Sparkles?"

"A dark shape that sparkles," I said.

He nodded, but I wasn't entirely certain that he could understand exactly what I meant in English.

"Our witches are real, but they are not really witches," he said.

"That's one way to put it."

"You must understand something," he said. "The most remote cavalry outposts in the Roman Empire were located only a few hours' drive east and north of this area. This is where the first people lived in Europe, long before even the Romans. These are pre-Christian rituals. There is no harm in the witches who live—can you say this?—in our midst."

"That's grammatically correct," I said.

"It's natural to play games with foreigners," he said. "A trick of the eye. No harm intended."

"You're saying witches live in the forest? I thought maybe you would offer me some antidepressant pills."

"Pills," he smirked, waving away the idea with his hand. "These only serve the 'placebo effect.' One thing that's wrong with you is that you are unemployed. Therefore, you have no world."

"No world?" I said.

The words rang true, but I wasn't certain I understood exactly what he meant.

"No . . . anchoring points . . . no harbor, if you prefer. You must make a friend—"

"—Of horror?" I interrupted.

"What does this mean, please?"

"It's a line from a movie. 'You must make a friend of horror.' Marlon Brando. *Apocalypse Now.*"

"Make a friend of horror?"

"Yes," I said. "Like, you must acquaint yourself with terrible things and witness the worst imaginable happenings. Something like that."

"Oh, no," he said, adjusting his glasses and looking very concerned. "No, no, no."

The glasses had lime green frames and were held to his neck by a chain. Suddenly he snapped them apart—they were designed to lock together at the center by magnets when on the nose and to rest in two separate pieces on the neck.

"You're having a _____ ," he said.

The word was German, lengthy, and compounded of many smaller words. Undoubtedly there was at least one umlaut in there. I nodded, making a mental note to ask him to write it down.

"Yes, a _____," he continued. "It's nothing to laugh at."

"Was I laughing?"

"No, but laughter really is the best medicine," he said. "I read this in your *Readers' Digest* on the base at Frankfurt where all of your fellow American sickos live with their bombers."

"What would you do if you were me?" I said.

"Isn't it 'were I'?"

"Um, I don't know. Maybe?"

"English is such a mess," he said. "You don't even know the answer."

"I'm sorry."

"You mention this old love affair with a person who is clearly 'out to lunch,'" he said, actually using scare quotes around the phrase. "Not to mention these projections of evil on harmless local traditions and fairy tales. Somebody has been reading the Brothers Grimm!"

"You're saying she's the problem?"

"Not she but your image of she—of her? She's what's inside your head. You still love her, but this makes you feel bad. I suggest you fuck your wife a little bit more often. Or find another person to fuck."

"Start an affair?" I said. "That's your medical advice?"

"These sanitized and melodramatic American sexual mores do not concern me. Your body is dying from a lack of sexual charge and this corrodes your brain."

"Is that a medical diagnosis?"

"I'm sorry to put it to you in a vulgar way, but a good German blond of any gender would have you patched up within a week. I can recommend a swingers' website. We meet out in the woods."

"We? So it's witches and orgies, then? That's the local culture?"

"We're living in the middle of nowhere," he remarked,

raising his eyebrows to emphasize his point. "I'm really just trying to shock you a little bit. Americans are so uptight."

"Noted."

"Death begins inside and works its way out," he said. "Surely you must have noticed this? Take some action before your private organs start to go sour."

"Do you have some scholarly literature on this condition?"

"It's common sense," he said. "You're lonely and you are externalizing the contents of your rotten mind."

"You might be right about that," I said.

"Taste some local honey," he observed as he showed me to the door.

"Are you insane?" I said.

"See, you're feeling better already," he smirked. "Enjoy your stay in Germany and give some thought to everything I've said. Having a lover is the only reliable method for picking up a second language as an adult. How otherwise will you learn your datives? And please don't use words like 'insane'; it's disrespectful of a serious condition."

"This has been extraordinarily unhelpful, doctor."

"I'm so glad," he said. "You see, I don't really think much of Americans. Imagine having the arrogance to look down on others after everything you've done."

"Okay," I said.

"You're not even able to muster nationalistic anger," he said. "Maybe you really are clinically depressed. I'm glad! You deserve it."

Amidst his hostility I had forgotten to ask the doctor to write down the German name for my condition. Was something about "wandering" contained within the long compound word he'd used, or had I misheard?

As bizarre and inappropriate as his advice had been, the doctor was right about one thing. Amy was a death trap. Amy herself wouldn't have denied it. In fact, that was her own claim. She was inviting me to spiral down with her. I resolved not to contact her again. Of course, I had said that to myself before.

I had another peculiar encounter when I arrived at our flat after walking up the hill from the hospital. Our building manager was Italian, I think, and he wore a traditional Tyrolean cap. I found him operating the locks on the front door to the complex, which was often sticky and sometimes unreliable. Some of the residents tended to prop it open during the day.

"Do you have a child?" he asked, in English, without greeting me first.

"No. Why?"

"We've had reports of a child screaming late at night in the building. You heard this."

I had—the kid had woken me up several times—but I thought nothing of it. I assumed it must have been an American couple sleep training their child, or something like that. The idea of sleep training was to let the kid shriek until they realized that nobody was coming to comfort them. The theory was that they would then go to sleep. I found this idea terrifying, perhaps because it implied a worldview in which everyone had to learn to be alone.

For some reason I decided to lie to the building manager, maybe simply because he had not greeted me.

"I heard nothing," I said, in German.

"The investigation," he replied, in English, "reveals that there is no child registered as living in this building."

"I don't understand," I said.

He looked at me pointedly, with a steadiness that alarmed me.

"We seek out explanations for these noises," he said, in English. "Our records reflect that no child is here. Zero kids. How could it be?"

Then he went into a long German sentence with a lot of lengthy words in it. Something about things meaning something or maybe about his impression that things were supposed to mean something but that things did not mean anything after all.

"I'm sorry?" I said, in German.

"Everyone has complained about this screaming child except for you," he said. "Don't you consider that suspicious?"

I shrugged and went inside, where nobody was home, feeling discombobulated by my chat with Amy and my encounters with the doctor and the building manager. No new mysterious packages awaited me. I had nothing to do but keep on reading Amy's manuscript while I waited for Rebecca to arrive home. Checking our bedroom, I saw no signs that she had been in the flat at all over the last twenty-four hours. I wondered if Amy had left me any clues for me to read, so I opened to a random page:

My Madeleines. *This is also the story of Kim Novak herself, and every other star in our lives, literal or metaphorical, public or private, far-off or near at hand. The deadly fixation that comes only to the unlucky people picked out for our attention and celebrity stalking. The obsessive object of desire, the death-trip glamour-puss with the muscular neck that induces strangulation fantasies. The cords on Joan Fontaine's neck. Grace Kelly's neck. Janet Leigh's neck. Get the picture? The person who is not allowed to be a per-*

*son. Whichever blond happens to be in your imaginary ho-
tel room, emerging from the green light of a neon memory
like a ghost. Didn't Kim Novak have a mustache? Maybe
there is another way to watch these movies. Wouldn't it be
interesting to watch someone slice into your neck? If you
didn't want to see a murder, why did you come to the cinema? Why didn't you leave—or simply avert your eyes?
This is a story about possession. This is a film about turning
a person into a possession. We retain a trophy in the form of
a corpse. Films about sex and murder. Spiral out from those
dead blue eyes, those still wet eyelashes. But now I am confusing my blonds.*

Reading these lines, I saw myself the way that Amy must
have seen me: the blond with the strong neck and the blue
eyes that must be extinguished. Maybe Amy had fantasized about my death and now she wanted me to publish
these notes as my own, as if she inhabited my insides. She
wanted the world to think that I saw what she saw. It was
the eclipse of my own separate identity, our merging in
her domination. I wanted to object. There were other ways
to make a work of art, and good reasons to see things differently. Possession, that's not love. Amy had confused
role-play for something else because she refused to ask
for my permission. In that moment, I felt more sorry for

Amy than I felt afraid for myself. I cared about her, and she was very ill. Then the fear returned again, along with everything Amy had said about our lives being in danger. Where was Amy? Where was Rebecca?

Then the child began to scream again, somewhere nearby in the building. Was it the same voice? The kid sounded utterly frantic, like they were being tortured slowly. I wanted to get away from the sound and find the building manager so that he could confirm the location of the child. But I couldn't find him anywhere, and I didn't want to go back into our flat, so I set off into the forest, hoping to clear my head. It was now or never—if I didn't face my fears squarely, I wasn't sure I would ever leave the house again. It would just be me and Amy's book and the screaming child and waiting for Rebecca forever. I had to go back into the woods and see if I could figure out what was happening. It didn't matter what I saw out there. It couldn't have been any worse than the contents of the mirror.

SIX

I passed by the allotments overlooking the mountains and found the electrical box with the MDEAD graffiti and the upside-down cross. I stood closer to examine the tag, realizing that I should have done an image search to see where else the design had appeared. The tag would have been unremarkable in any city, but out here, at the edge of the old forest where people probably had been living for tens of thousands of years, where the local psychiatrist claimed that witches practiced their craft, it stuck out amidst the spandex-clad bicyclists, huffing joggers, horse girls, and older couples walking hand in hand or with their trekking poles.

Still, this was Germany. Black metal and pagan vibes and werewolf enclaves couldn't be ruled out. Paranoia reached out its tentacles, responding to the call of an older darkness I imagined underlying the body-culture-crazed, seven-grain-bread-worshiping, too-good-to-be-true recycling theocracy of learned Tübingen.

Some sort of equal and opposite reaction to the splintering official cultural slogans of tolerance, a deeper and more sinister polarity that lay hidden from public view but remained haunted and energized to reactivate itself when the time was right, like the half-suppressed knowledge I grew up with in the American Midwest related to Wisconsin's Indian reservations or the 1930s Volksbund rallies at Camp Hindenburg, outside Milwaukee, as "Friends of New Germany." Time travel, bilocation— Amy was obviously correct in one sense about the interconnected web of doppelgänger places, I could be here and there, then and now. The placards in Tübingen depicting the Nazi rallies along the riverside down in town reminded me that these events had happened within living memory, for some, and within a generation or two for much of the population. Parents or grandparents who had resisted, remained silent, turned amnesiac, passively complied, spoke up, or become active saboteurs. Where were you in '42?

Late afternoon sun illuminated the inner processes of the forest, dappling the trails lovingly in brightness and shadow, like a painter of wonderful nature clichés. Wind blew heavily through the pines and birches, making a calming sound of such tranquility that I almost forgot Amy's words from earlier about looking for a tree that looked like a tree but was not a tree. Was this some kind of riddle, a LARPing game she had cooked up to entertain and scare me, the world's strangest gift?

All dark woods should feel the same in any language, but they are not. This was a German forest, which meant that it was both utilitarian and mystical, with logging roads and monastery villages inside it, appearing much larger to the explorer on foot than it was in reality. Nothing about it was truly wild, but everything in here seemed slightly weird and off-kilter to me as a foreigner, as though things were inhabiting the present and the past simultaneously. I found newly harvested pine trunks pungent with names, numbers, and initials spray painted on them, "Grünewald" and "R.P.," stacked next to a small grove of mossy birches that looked elfin and medieval in their size and wisdom. The park was tamer and yet more mysterious than any American woods where centuries of continuous inhabitation had been erased. No impression of wilderness was being attempted. Walkers chatted away on their cell phones on well-groomed trails of gravel strewn with oak acorns. The trails had been here for decades, if not longer, and the footpaths down into the valley with the monastery had existed for hundreds of years. Aside from the mice and the hawks that fed on them, a few hares and deer, and the rumored wild boar that snuffled in the corners of the park, the woods held very little life apart from birdsong, which emanated from everywhere. Nowhere should have felt safer and more mellow than this walk among the knots of drunken students dragging backpacks crammed with beer through the hills. Hunting traps lined the ridges, establishing watching posts up in the trees where someone could see and not be seen.

A solitary figure passed me on the trail, looking up to meet my eyes directly and boldly. Black hoodie, weathered backpack, closely cropped green hair, plump, rectangular heavy-framed glasses, violet eyes with some dew in them and a fierce intelligence. She was wearing a bandanna around her face with a skull printed on it. It covered her neck, mouth, and nose, leaving those piercing eyes, magnified by the lenses of her glasses, regarding me above the skeleton cheekbones and jaw. I nodded but she only looked through me. Once she passed by on the narrow trail, she turned, briefly, so that her skull-face looked back at me. I took a side trail deeper into the woods, away from the sunlight.

The trees themselves were somehow unnerving in their splendor. I had never seen deciduous trees growing this tall in such numbers. The birches in particular had been spared the ax. Their lichen-spotted bark grew from mossy trunks into cathedral rows flanking the paths and creating a green shade canopy through which—*stimmung, Nosferatu*—the half-clouded light filtered like an aura from another era or another world. Mist appeared as the sun fell. The mist looked like smoke from tiny campfires, but in fact it was created by the specific atmospherics of the place, sun-heated plants exhaling into cool overcast mountain evenings.

The witches I had been warned about by my unhelpful doctor—The Doktor, as I thought of him, like the villain in a silent German horror movie—lived or did not live out here. The skull-faced woman was meeting with the coven—probably not. Our Lady of Sighs breathing her spells, like the Black Forest creature that lives on blood in the school for dancers in *Suspiria*. That was in Freiburg, not a million miles away from here, but a different and even more haunted woods. I pictured the film's opening, with Jessica Harper playing Suzy Bannion, a frightened but brave American girl, just arrived in Germany for ballet training, traversing the dark woods in a taxi in a chilling rainstorm, the windows streaked with Technicolor lights, a flash of lightning suddenly exposing a view from outside the car, the forest silhouetted, the beams of the cab slicing the downpour, and a dark shape quivering on a tree trunk. The soundtrack's repeating whisper-scream of "Witch!"

I retraced my steps back to our building and then took a different path into the Naturpark, across the soybean and wheat fields, past a farm and a side path leading to a small soccer stadium, before descending back down into the forest, skirting a large purple building that I'd read was a Waldorf school. In a clearing near a parking lot, gnarled oaks centuries old towered over VWs, an abandoned couch, and a cell-tower station bristling with antennae made to look vaguely like tree branches. Was this the tree that wasn't a tree? I remembered that I hadn't turned off my phone, but it was useless without Wi-Fi, receiving no data. I started hunting around the concrete base of the tower and even tried the door of the little building embedded in the concrete, but everything was locked, and the signs said something about electricity and death. A little road threaded the forest, taking cars down into the valley to the monastery town. Ten yards from the road, deserted paths carved deeper into

the forest that stretched nearly to the suburbs of Stuttgart. A placard map with legends I could not read stood
near the entrance to the path, although the symbols were
clear enough.

I must have been imagining things, before, under the
influence of my loneliness and nerves, projecting fear
onto the faces of these harmless trees that lived only to
exchange carbon for oxygen. These were the woods that
Höderlin had treated as an oracular force, suggesting that
poets ask Nature for advice. The poet mocked those who
claimed that the Earth was dead, just a lifeless set of ob-
jects to be manipulated and harvested for human util-
ity. (But what if the Earth was undead?) If the forest held
witches, they had to be the real kind, the good kind, pow-
erful shamans with curative spells, resisting the patriar-
chy and dedicated to healing plants, as the doctor had
hinted. My spirits rose out of the depths whenever I was
inhaling oak leaves and wild garlic, everything that did
not reek of diesel or require air-conditioning to survive
the heat in a concrete box.

Every step marked: getting lost wasn't possible in the
crisscrossing networks of trails, and nothing you could
see hadn't been seen by ten thousand other walkers
over the years and decades and centuries and millennia.
Maybe when the Nazis held their rallies down in town;

these trees also hid little pockets of resistance meetings. If there were witches here, they cast their spells against fascism, surely, mindful of other eras when everyone odd or unusual got hunted down.

I had been thinking about everything the wrong way. I felt drugged by the trees, it was almost an experience of levitation, the yearning to love all witches and to have a spell cast on me. I descended deeper into the forest, into the valley between the folding ridges with a ribbon of paved bike path traversing a small stream. According to the placard map, it would lead me to the monastery that was said to lie at the precise geographical center of this province and former kingdom. My gloom lifted as my muscles tired and my feet started to feel slightly swollen in my sneakers. It seemed funny that I had ever thought that someone or something could be following me. Why would anyone bother?

This wasn't nature, but rather an extension of a German mode of thinking about the health effects of being outdoors. A little terrarium for people to enjoy, like a toy sunken ship at the bottom of a fish tank, a playground for us goldfish to nose around, so to speak. Nature—real nature—was vast and terrifying. Nature was the double-asteroid hit that had smashed the land for miles in the Swabian plains eons ago, creating a crater so wide that an entire town had been built inside of its circumference. The natural life was the one depicted in the university museum. It involved cowering in a cave during thunderstorms, carving lion-people and flutes from mastodon ivory, after figuring out a method for killing this creature many times larger than oneself without getting maimed or trampled to death in the process. No, this park was picture-postcard stuff, a figment of the Teutonic imagination about the nature of nature.

But then I thought of a painting I'd seen in Stuttgart, Otto Dix's *The Triumph of Death*. The museum held two rooms of Dix's nightmares, painted by an artist among the first to be dismissed from their teaching posts by the National Socialist regime after they had consolidated their grip on power. In the painting, Death wielded his scythe over a tableau comprising a German soldier with a fixed bayonet, an old woman who searched in vain on the ground for something, a baby that looked freshly abandoned in a patch of flowers, a blind man who seemed to sense the advent of doom, and a voluptuous woman with long tresses being undressed by a dissolute young man. In the background of the painting stood snowcapped mountain peaks that resembled the areas of this region further south and east that bordered on Austria, the kind of place where Hitler built his Eagles' Nest fortress. Dix

knew what he was doing when he claimed those ideal-
ized mountains as the backdrop for terror. The Nazis cur-
dled the idea of fresh air, even. In the guise of the mountains, they offered trenches for corpses and pits stacked
with death, torture chambers, and chimneys. Dix had
seen it all, the face in the mountain, the potential killer
and the future victim, the witness who dares not to speak
and the person who fights back, the one who turns away
and the one who bends down to tend the wounded.

It was in another tiny village south of here—not distant by American standards—where a nuclear research
station had been built into the hills. Part of a secret project to weaponize atomic energy, an outpost that was now
a local museum hidden deep in the forests packed with
caves where the prehistoric flutes once played. It was difficult to hold these sets of images in mind together, the
chapel in the birches and the mushroom cloud, the blue
mists on the receding mountains and the death-scythe
of Allied bombs raining down on the shattered city of
Stuttgart. I had admired how the city had rebuilt itself
in modern blocks rather than attempting the meticulous
reconstructions imitating past glory in Dresden. In that
reconstituted toy city of the firestorms, the far-right was
active on their Monday marches, whereas wrecked Stuttgart favored the garish style of a 1950s department store
look that I found charming in its banality.

A series of coughs behind me drew my attention to the figure walking behind me towards the monastery town, some fifty yards away. It was difficult to tell at this distance if it was the same person I'd seen earlier, but I thought I recognized the black hoodie. When I turned to look, the figure took down the hoodie and revealed her green hair. She was no longer wearing the skull-face bandanna and now she looked like any other grad student on a stroll.

When I slowed down my pace slightly, she dawdled to tie the shoelaces of her patent-leather boots or pretended to take an interest in a flowering tree by the side of the path.

In Bebenhausen, the medieval monastery in the dream-village was closed and emanating classical music by the time I reached it. They let visitors walk the grounds past the cemetery and the grassy park around the village castle walls. I wandered the ridiculously quaint footpaths around the houses and gardens in the little village, passing splendid arrays of flowers and a twee restaurant with an outdoor garden where classy-looking people in suits and evening gowns held flutes of champagne and motorcyclists sipped beers in colorful leathers.

The woman continued shadowing my steps at a polite distance, making her way through the same route, towards the footpath leading out of town and looping back towards Tübingen. It was a steep climb from the village, offering views of an impossibly perfect fairy-tale German town of peaked roofs and greenery. Whenever I stopped, she stopped as well, keeping her distance, but clearly keeping me in sight. Once we were out of town and back in the deserted woods, she put up her black hood again, and retied the skeleton face around her mouth and ears.

Closer to the edge of the woods, near the car park where I had searched around the cell phone tower, I started hearing shoes crushing acorns and gravel on the trail, then the sound of labored breathing behind me. I thought about running away, but I was already too tired to win this race—the woman clearly had fresher legs. As she neared, the hair started rising on the back of my neck. I couldn't escape the feeling that this person knew me or wanted to exchange words with me.

Then I heard a sigh of recognition as the figure passed. She turned towards me without pausing and I saw her face. It wasn't the woman with the unnerving bandanna. It was my wife, jogging in place.

"Hello?" Rebecca said.

She was wearing a black nylon running hoodie with reflective zippers. I looked back down the hill to see if the other figure was there, the younger woman with green hair and glasses, but she was nowhere to be seen.

"Did you pass someone wearing a skull-face bandanna back there?"

"I was focused on my run," Rebecca said, her breathing calming, the sweat on her long curling neck looking almost ornamental, her legs arcing gloriously into her gym-honed calves beneath spandex.

"Think you can keep up?" she said, continuing to run into place so as not to lose her rhythm.

"No," I said. "My feet hurt. I think somebody's following me."

She frowned and winced, as if I'd said something very strange or stupid.

"Need me to carry you back to the flat?" she said.

"I'll just take it easy," I said. "I thought you were someone else."

"This person who's following you?"

"Do you think a person can be in two places at once?" I asked. "Where have you been?"

Rebecca shrugged, smiled thinly, and bounded off through the forest like a fox, giving me a little wave. She was shapely and lithe, and with a marathoner's sleek but slightly shriveled body and strong muscular legs. I had to laugh at myself, inwardly, for ogling my wife, but her beauty actually wasn't my type. She was almost out of earshot when she turned and shouted two words back in my direction:

"Remote entanglement!"

With that, she sprinted away from me towards the

clearing where the wheat and soybean fields began. Clearly she wanted to avoid discussing her overnight absence. Maybe if I rushed home I could ask her about it, but I wasn't sure I wanted to know the answers to my questions, or maybe I already knew the answers in my heart of hearts. I looked around me into the woods and tried to listen for any sign of the green-haired stalker, but she seemed to have vanished.

When I finally picked my way across the fields to our apartment, slowed by rising blisters, Rebecca was already gone. She must have showered quickly and caught a bus down into town for a glass of wine with her colleagues, or whoever it was that she was spending her time with now in the evenings. She *really* didn't want to have that discussion about her whereabouts. I could try trolling the university bars until I found her, but I dreaded the motion sickness of the buses. Besides, what purpose would be served by confronting her? Clearly she wanted to be left the fuck alone.

I pulled the blinds and heated up some soup, then settled into bed with the excesses of Amy's manuscript, convinced that there might be a clue in there somewhere about what was happening. Some part of me missed her intensity. Above our bed a window looked out on an outdoor staircase that carried students down to the bus stop. The streetlamp at the top of the staircase cast shadows of figures into our bedroom and carried their voices in the cool night air. The part of the window that could be opened was high enough that it couldn't be reached from ground level—a clever German design—but the window itself went all the way down to the floor. There was a double curtain, but I thought that if someone really wanted to, they could stand in the gravel outside the window and press their ear against the glass and listen to what was happening in the room. Sometimes when I drew open the curtain in the morning, I half-expected to see a face at the window looming in front of me like some kind of deranged mirror. Across a small courtyard, another concrete tower of flats rose above our bedroom. With the curtains open, people could look in and see our bed, and, in turn, we could overhear the conversations and the singing and the drinking games of the graduate students who lived across the way.

I rifled through the pages of Amy's book, reading passages at random. Having digested enough of it to see the fuller picture, her manuscript appeared to be a journal of disconnected notes written after multiple viewings of *Vertigo*. The work was clearly incomplete and in some

places it didn't make sense to me. One page in the middle
of the book read:

> **Scottie, *C'est Moi*.** *What really happened during Scottie's
> fugue state, after believing that he's seen his forbidden lover
> Madeleine throw herself from the church's bell tower? This
> scene is "cut" from the film, but it would reveal everything.
> The film would have us believe that he never approaches her
> dead body. Therefore, he never notices that the corpse isn't
> the same person he has been following around San Fran-
> cisco. He never realizes that this is not the woman with
> whom he's fallen in love. In his state of shock, Scottie drives
> himself all the way home to San Francisco without realizing
> what he's doing. Why does he do this? How does he survive
> the journey without crashing his car? Does he do anything
> else he cannot remember on this trip? Scottie clearly blames
> himself for Madeleine's death. He thinks he has let her die,
> and, in his mind, he is fleeing the scene of the crime as if* he
> *were the murderer. (Hitchcock captures the strange truth
> that we are guilty for all the things we have* not *done.)* Ver-
> tigo *follows the logic of a dream. Hitchcock found out what
> Krampf and Murnau discovered years earlier about the land
> of phantoms. Movies are dreams that remind us the world
> itself isn't real. Only the movies are real, and only when we
> enter into a movie do we really live. That is why the silly an-*

imated dream sequence, during which Scottie's severed head
falls through Carlotta's grave into the blackness of darkness
forever, is the most important and the most realistic scene
in Vertigo. *I know where Scottie went on his drive. Into a*
time machine.

I began to drift off while reading Amy's notes, which I
found increasingly difficult to follow. Did she want me to
embellish them and straighten out her manuscript into a
more ordered arrangement, performing the role of copy
editor? As long as Amy allowed me to remove my name
from her book, which was all her. It would need to be
published as fiction.

Reading about dreams, my brain hatched its own
branching paths of narratives as I sank down into the pillows, exhausted from my walk and convinced that Rebecca would not return that night. I dreamed about a
postcard German village, which I encountered after a
long walk in the woods. The village was like Bebenhausen but was not Bebenhausen and the trees in the woods
surrounding the town were like trees, but they were not
trees. From a distance, the decay and abandonment in the
dream village hadn't been obvious at first. But as I wandered in the cobbled streets I found the windows of the
houses broken and the shutters hanging askew, the paint

peeling from the wattle and the roof tiles scattered in dis-
array on the ground. Nobody lived there.

I came upon a sign with a single, absurdly long compound German word printed on it—so long that the word
was separated into several lines and arranged in smaller
pieces by dashes so that it could fit on the sign. It was the
name of the dream town, which was not Bebenhausen.
Some parts of the long word felt familiar, but I couldn't
place them exactly. I think it was the name of the disease
that the German doctor had ascribed to me. According
to the logic of the dream, it only took me a few minutes
of walking in the town for me to understand that I was
suffering from radiation sickness, with multiple tumors
pulsing under my abdomen. I also knew, somehow, that
I was in World War Two and that the Allies had dropped
the Bomb on this town in Southern Germany due to the
Nazis' failure to surrender. It was 1946 and the battles had
kept going beyond the point of military defeat. The German civilians had not accepted the occupation and had
endorsed an insurgency campaign instead. I had drifted
into an exclusion zone.

I had the idea of escaping from the radiation by climbing as far as I could into the bell tower of the village
church, where ravens had gathered hideously deformed
mice with multiple heads and tails for a deranged feast

that would kill the birds soon after they ate the tainted meat. As I looked down over the town—my location shifted very quickly from ground level to the top of the spire without seeming to climb any stairs—I saw that the season had somehow turned to winter in the blink of an eye. Snow fell into the deepening gloom at the horizon and another line of ravens descended on a spot outside the village where something lay maimed and bleeding in the snow. I thought I recognized the corpse as my own.

Even within the dream, I knew this image for its resemblance with another painting by Otto Dix, featuring a village where nothing was out of place, but everything was wrong. I floated down over the village inside the painting, gently tumbling like a dying moth. I could not remember if I was pushed from the church or if I had jumped. My motion sickness had been completely cured by the fall, I realized, to my great (but temporary) joy. But I saw I only had a few moments left on Earth, and I realized that the snowflakes were ashes.

I woke up alone in the dead of night to the sound of someone tapping at our bedroom window.

SEVEN

The curtains were closed, so the tapping at the glass could be dismissed as a tree branch (although there were no trees outside our window). Possibly it was a little bit of blown trash that had somehow stuck to the windowpane (although it sounded like a human fingernail). It might have been any number of things that could be imagined as long as I left the curtains shut. But the tapping persisted, in little bursts, like Morse code, three taps, then two taps. Tap-tap-tap. Tap-tap. Rebecca hadn't returned. Was she locked out? I lay stock-still in bed, hoping whoever was out there would conclude that nobody was home and go away. Instead the tapping grew louder, as if the figure at the window was using their knuckle instead of their fingernail now.

Finally, I drew the curtain and saw Amy's face, except that she looked slightly different, as if she had put on a little weight and reversed the aging process. She was wearing blockish personality glasses and had dyed her hair green. Except it wasn't her. It was the young woman with the skull-face bandanna who had followed me through the woods. But it was also Amy, a younger version of her, anyway. This was impossible but it was what I saw.

I hadn't thought I would ever see Amy again. Amy/ Not Amy looked as unhappy as ever and unwell around the eyes. Backlighting from the streetlamp made the circles under her eyes look bruised. She held herself awkwardly as if she were in a considerable amount of pain. I opened the top of the window so that we could speak. Cool air seeped in with the sweet smell of the small hours in summer.

"You're shivering," she said, sounding like she'd traveled light-years. "I'm not here to hurt you. It's cold out. Where are we?"

"Germany," I said, stupidly.

"I want to go into the woods."

"Come in and warm up," I said. "I'll meet you at the patio door."

"I saw your wife!" she said, looking startled, then closing her eyes as if she'd seen something she wished she hadn't. "She was . . . not okay."

"She's not here now," I said. "You can come in if you want."

"No, follow me," she said. "I'm sorry."

Amy/Not Amy turned away and headed towards the concrete outdoor stairs and the footpath that led toward the fields and the forest. I threw on shorts and shoes and raced as fast as I could to the patio entrance without tying the laces. As I exited the flat, I heard the door lock behind me with a click and realized that I had forgotten the key. I didn't see Amy/Not Amy anywhere in the courtyard, so I climbed the stairs and ran up the street towards the entrance to the Naturpark. She seemed to have disappeared. I jogged a few dozen yards into the woods and quickly stumbled into some tree roots, taking a fall that I could feel had bloodied my knees and left my ears ringing with pain. Inside the canopy of trees, no light emanated from the forest. I kept bumping into shrubs and low branches. Progress felt impossible—were the trees moving?—so I retraced my steps and tried the path into the wheat fields instead. At first I whispered Amy's name, but then I lost any sense of self-control and began shouting for her. A few lights in the blocks of flats flicked on as I continued moving along the road shrieking.

The woods had nothing to say. The stars illuminated nothing. The night was dead. A horrible thought dawned on me, obvious in retrospect but shocking to me at the time. I had dreamed the face at the window. Amy had never been here. It wasn't possible.

Dispirited, I walked back to our building, wondering how on earth I would get in without my key. The building manager's flat was on the ground floor, but I hesitated because it was after 2 am. After some hemming and hawing, I rang his bell, once, twice, then incessantly. After a minute or two, a light popped on. Eventually he answered, wearing a dressing gown and his Tyrolean hat. He was not happy to see me.

"I forgot my keys," I said. "I'm terribly sorry."

He looked me over, noticing my bloody knees and palms. He whisked me into the building and turned to go, but I told him I needed him to unlock the door to our flat as well.

"Isn't your wife in?" he said.

I shook my head.

"Oh," he said, beaming for the first time in our interactions.

We were in the darkened hallway outside our door, and he was turning his master key in the lock to our flat when we both heard it. The screaming child for which he had no record of living in the building started cry-ing again. The kid sounded like they were being burned alive, but then again, that's also how little kids tend to sound when they're throwing a tantrum, and every small agony feels like a matter of life or death.

"Strange," the building manager said, "It sounds like it's coming from over there."

He pointed in the darkness to a door to a storage area adjacent to our flat. I knew that nobody lived there—it was essentially a crawl space with a little door that was never locked. I had nosed into this little room when we'd first moved in, and found it stuffed to the gills with stacks of office chairs. The building manager flicked on the timed lights in the hallway and we both moved to-wards the door of the storage closet, where the screaming child seemed to be hiding.

When he opened the door, the screaming inside qua-drupled in volume. The kid was being drawn and quar-tered now, from the sound of it. It was that hideous cry that no human being could hear without rushing to the child's aid.

The building manager and I barely fit into the storage room together because it was so packed full of chairs. He turned on another light inside the little room. As far as I could see, the room held nothing but chairs. The screaming sound came from below the stacks of chairs on the side of the room that shared a wall with our bedroom. The sound emanated from a spot that was only a few feet away from where Rebecca laid her head to sleep on the other side of the wall, on nights she slept at home. The building manager and I started removing chairs as quickly as we could to get to the noise.

After a few minutes of work, we finally uncovered the source of the screaming. It wasn't a demonic crib. We found ourselves staring down at an old-fashioned tape recorder that was playing back the sound of the shrieking. The tapes inside the recorder were magnetic analogue, wheeled by mechanical sprockets. While we stood there watching, the screaming stopped abruptly, although we saw the tape spools keep on turning. There were intervals of silence built into this program.

"Who would do such a thing?" he said, furrowing his brow.

He bent down to shut off the machine, but I held his arm back.

"Fingerprints," I said. "This is a police matter."

"Call them in the morning," he said. "It's not an emergency."

He led me back to our door and let me into our flat.

"Whoever did this has a master key to the building," I said.

"Not necessarily," the building manager said. "The front door is often open during the day and that little room is never locked."

I nodded and thanked him, pointlessly. He touched my arm near my shoulder and turned to go, but I held up a finger for him to wait while I brought him a large half-liter bottle of Paulaner. When the building manager was gone, I opened a second bottle for myself, put earplugs in, and moved my pillows and blankets to the couch in the living room by the patio door, as far as it was possible to go in our flat away from the wall that adjoined the storage room. There I counted the hours, failed to sleep, saw Amy's words swimming in front of my eyes, wondered what exactly had happened with the face at the window, chewed over why anyone would want to place recordings of screaming children next to our flat, and worried about my wife, about us.

The next morning—in truth it was getting on towards noon—I was awakened by a sparkling-eyed policewoman with henna-red hair tucked neatly into a baseball cap with intimidating-looking official insignias stitched into the peak.

"I rang the bell," she said, in English, sniffing the bad air before opening the patio door to create a small breeze in the heat of midday. "The building manager let me in."

"Oh," I said, still very groggy, gathering the duvet around me in a makeshift attempt to hide my bare chest and boxers, wincing as the heavy fabric scraped across my scabby knees where the blood from my forest adventure had dried during sleep.

"Your wife is reported missing," she said. "Get dressed and prepare to answer some questions."

I rose, holding the duvet around me like a robe, and retreated into the bedroom for some sweatpants and a hoodie. I could use the pockets to hide my scraped palms, but I didn't know why it mattered to me to disguise my injuries.

EIGHT

"You are concerned," the policewoman stated, rather than asking, as she stirred a cup of tea she had made for herself in our kitchen while I was dressing. Presumably she'd had a look around the fridge and the sink to see whether she could determine if two people had been eating and washing up here in recent days.

"Concerned?" I said. "Do you mean 'worried' or 'involved'?"

"What an odd question!" she said, looking away towards the window.

"Who reported her missing? That seems very fast."

"A colleague," she said. "She wasn't in her lecture hall this morning, and nobody knew how to reach you by telephone. We like to be seen as responsive to the university. So here I am."

"There isn't a telephone here," I said.

"My first question is this. Why did't *you* report her missing?"

"She hasn't been gone long enough," I said. "Isn't there a forty-eight-hour waiting period over here?"

"It looks like she hasn't been here in a couple of days, based on what I've seen in the kitchen."

"She showered here yesterday," I said. "But the answer to your question is embarrassing. I think she's taken up with someone else."

"How long has she been gone?"

"I saw her yesterday, but she hasn't been here regularly for a few days."

"This is not serious for you," the policewoman said.

"*Doch!*" I said, attempting a German word that I wasn't sure I was using correctly, and wondering if I had said the opposite of what I meant. "It would be serious for me if I did not take it seriously."

The policewoman frowned. I suspected that her English, though impeccable on the surface, was not enough to grasp fully what I meant, but that she wished to keep

me at ease in this interview situation by remaining polite. I could tell that she was interviewing me with multiple purposes and with various alternatives in mind. She
had a habit of tapping the rim of the tea mug with her
fingernails, which were unpolished, chipped, and well-
gnawed. The dye in her hair seemed to be fading in a few
places.

"It is serious for me," I said, finally.

"I am thinking it is very serious for you!" she said, her
eyes sparkling.

I had absolutely no idea whether she meant that it was
serious for me because she suspected me of something or
if it was serious for me because she accepted that I felt the
matter required seriousness. So I tried not to contradict
her or appear nervous.

"Rebecca Clarke," she said. "Such a lovely American
name. We need a good photo. Mainly the face."

I retrieved my smartphone and turned it on so that
she could see Rebecca, one of the first images that came
up on my image gallery, a snapshot of Rebecca building a deck behind our house in Vermont overlooking the
mountains. It seemed like a different life, another person,
a previous existence, someone else's house, not my home,
not Rebecca, a foreign land. Only the mountains looked
somewhat similar to where I was now.

"She's really stunning!" the policewoman said.

She snapped a photo of the photo with her own phone.

"Someone here in Tübingen thinks so, too," I said.

"We'll use her faculty photo to search," she said. "So you saw her for the last time . . ."

"The last time?" I said.

"Sorry, you saw her last—or is it 'you last saw her'?"

"The second is clearer," I said, "but either is okay."

"You're not worried about your wife," she said, matter-of-factly.

"No," I said.

"No, you're not worried?"

"No," I said, "I *am* worried."

"So when you last saw her . . ."

"Yesterday afternoon," I said. "She was out jogging in the forest. You know that parking lot—the car park on the little road to Bebenhausen? She passed me on her run."

"You were out running together?" the policewoman asked, sipping her tea and watching me intently under the brim of her official cap.

She wore her uniform in a posture that presented the appearance of being relaxed but was deeply attentive. Her eyes fixed on various aspects of my face and body as if she were running me through a scanner or pinning a bug to cardboard.

"I don't run," I said, trying to speak very slowly and very clearly. "I was out walking. I had been in Bebenhausen, and I was headed back here. I saw my wife entirely by coincidence. By the time I had walked back, she had already gone out again."

"How do you know that she came here first before going out?"

"The shower had been used," I said. "The bathroom floor was wet. Nice-smelling things."

"So you weren't together," the policewoman said, nodding, but still puzzled.

"It depends on what you mean by 'together,'" I said, using the German word.

"You didn't ask her where she might be going?" the policewoman continued, in English.

"I honestly thought I would see her here," I said. "We had some things to discuss."

"Like where she had been recently, and with whom."

"Yes," I admitted.

"You suspected her of an affair, and you were violently angry," she suggested.

"I wouldn't put it that way," I said.

"Yes?"

"No."

"So, Rebecca—I like to use the names of the missing,"

the policewoman said. "Just to be clear. She didn't tell you where she was going, or with whom."

"With whom?" I repeated, noting the policewoman's impeccable grammar, that perfect German British English which no American ever used.

The policewoman paused to make a note in a reporter's-style flip notebook.

"Do you know what I've written down here?" she said. "It says that you avoided answering a direct question from a police officer."

"I think I already answered that I didn't know where she was going," I said.

"And yet you don't appear terribly concerned."

"Honestly, I think she's having a little frolic," I said. "Was any other member of the American Studies faculty 'missing' this morning along with my wife?"

The policewoman widened her eyes and flipped her notebook closed, removed her cap, and went back to nursing the cup of tea she had appropriated.

"She said something," I said. "Just before she ran off. I asked her if she thought a person could be in two places at once. I was making a hint that I knew she was having an affair. She replied by saying the words, 'remote entanglement.' Just that, and then she was gone."

"What does this mean, please?" the policewoman said, flipping her notebook back open.

"I don't know," I said, in German, then shifted back to English. "I think it's something to do with quantum mechanics, physics? It's about subatomic particles that have the property of being capable of existing in two places at once? I'm not an expert."

"Remote entanglement," she said.

"In English," I said, "the word 'entanglement' could also be another word for an affair. Is that helpful?"

"Perhaps," she said. "Now about this campaign of terror in this building about these recordings of screaming children. The manager mentioned this to me."

"Could it be connected?" I said. "Is that what you're saying?"

"It's something that we must ask ourselves," she said. "There was a man in Rebecca's past? Someone she had snubbed? A person with a violent streak? An ex-boyfriend who stalked her?"

"Not that I know about," I said.

"Enemies in the academic setting?"

"We live in Vermont," I said. "It would be a really long way to go to harass us. We don't know anyone here in Germany. The idea seems implausible."

"Yes," she said. "No one in the university community seems to know who *you* are."

"I don't socialize with her colleagues."

"Would you describe yourself as antisocial?" she asked.

"I suppose," I said.

"You've been sleeping on the couch for some days?" she asked, arching her eyebrows.

"No," I said. "I moved here last night because of those awful recordings of the screaming."

"Why didn't you turn off the tape?"

"Fingerprints?" I said.

"Is there anything else you wish to reveal?" she said. When I shook my head, she continued. "Pull up your sweatpants. Past your knees."

I did what she asked, and she surveyed my skinned kneecaps. The policewoman took another snapshot with her phone.

"What are you doing?" I asked.

"It's proof," she said.

"Of what?"

"I don't know yet," she said. "All I know is that you tried to hide these wounds from me when I arrived."

"I'd like to tell you what happened," I said. "But it's going to sound farfetched."

"Farfetched?"

"Strange?" I said. "Implausible?"

"I'm listening," she said.

I took a deep breath, and sought for some reassuring sign of eye contact, but the policewoman was glancing furtively at her phone.

"It must have been a dream," I said. "But in the middle of the night I heard tapping at my bedroom window, and when I drew the curtain I saw a face looking in at me. It was . . . an old lover of mine. Someone who lives in San Francisco now. It wasn't possible for her to be here."

The policewoman swung her laser eyes back towards me, locking on to my left eye. This was a trained response, I knew, to convey an impression of empathy. I told her how I thought I'd seen Amy—or a person who resembled Amy when she was younger—and how I'd stumbled out into the woods without my key, scraped myself up at the entrance to the forest, and then had to rouse the manager to get back inside because I was locked out of the building.

She asked to see the window where Amy's face—or the amalgam of Amy and the green-haired young woman (who I had left out of my story)—had appeared. The policewoman took out her notebook and started making a diagram of the window with a stick-like person at the glass. This surprised me because I had not thought that she would take me seriously.

She snapped some more photos of the window, then gave me a little thumbs up.

"What do you see?" I asked.

"Look, fingerprints, on the outside," she said, looking over our sad bed. "Confirms your story. Could you describe this person? The old lover, as you call her?"

"Amy."

"Would you describe Amy as unbalanced or violent in any way?"

I had to laugh, a little bit, at that.

"This is getting personal," I said. "I suppose she's a little . . . uh . . ."

"It's better for me to know."

"Okay," I said. "I'd say she was self-destructive. Possibly suicidal. She did hit me with a block of wood, once. But . . . I think she thought I would like it."

"During sex, you mean?"

"It was . . . I was going to say it was consensual. Mostly. Maybe."

"Was it?"

"I don't know how to describe it. It's not as though I couldn't have gotten away if I'd wanted to. Physically I was stronger. So."

"Did you?"

"What?"

"Like it?"

"I . . . I don't know what to say."

"You're a little bit mixed up," she said, looking at me very intently. "It's okay to be vanilla. Or to explore whatever's your thing."

"Are those official police policies?"

"Yes, and it's nothing to joke about," she said. "I'm into the dark shit, myself. Metal cop sex. By prior agreement, only, and for maximum extreme mutual pleasure. Quote unquote. Does that help? Sometimes sharing these things helps. It's not some moral aberration to mock or take fright about. Enough American Puritan bullshit. It's about consent, full stop."

She gestured towards her neck and pretended to yank a collar.

"I don't know," I said. "Do I have to know?"

"Have you ever used the internet?" she said. "Have you ever been to Berlin? You're in Germany. Go for it! Find your dick. Are you a Pisces by any chance?"

"This is not helping," I said.

"Yes, it is," she smiled, but then her look changed. "Listen to me. Without consent, it's abuse. You must know that."

I smiled back, weakly. It was helping, but I didn't want to admit it.

"Do you have a pamphlet or something?" I said.

"Actually, I do," she said. "But it's in German. Do you have reason to believe this person, Amy, might wish to do you harm, in a manner that is either imminent and extreme or continuous and ongoing?"

"It wasn't like that," I said. "But she did say that she thought something—someone—was following her and trying to kill her. And . . ."

"Yes?"

"She believed that whatever it was that was following her was also here, in the woods."

"That's different," she said.

"Amy had spent some time here, years ago."

"In Tübingen?"

"She thought that she'd seen something in the woods that was following her back then and maybe might also be following me right now. I know how that sounds."

"Perhaps," the policewoman said, narrowing her eyes, then looking away for a moment. "You never know. The woods are well-known to be haunted. Maybe that is not the right word. And maybe leave it there for now. But we should check and see if Amy is really where she says she is. Maybe she's traveled over here to disrupt your life."

"I don't see that as fitting her style," I said. "I haven't done a very good job of explaining our relationship."

"Maybe that's because you don't understand your own death drive," the policewomen said. "You look forward to being punished for crimes you haven't committed due to your personality. Or else you are expressing your own guilt for a crime you have committed, and in a very odd way. I think the former is more likely. Why don't you report these things?"

"What things?"

"All of them," she said. "Your wife's gone missing, people are terrorizing you with recordings of screaming, and then there's someone looking into your bedroom at night. This appears to be targeted harassment."

"The police are different in America," I said. "You don't talk to them. Ever."

"They're not that different anywhere," she said. "I might find a new job. What's that expression from the movies? 'Help me help you'?"

"Did you speak to the building manager?" I said.

"Of course," she said, as if I were questioning her professionalism. "He suspects you of abducting and murdering your wife. He's dumb as bread, but this cannot be ruled out yet. He did reveal something. You never reported the screaming child?"

"Why should I?"

"Even after you and he discovered the tape recordings in that little room down the corridor, you never called the police."

"What would that have accomplished?"

"It goes in our records," she said. "Then we have a full accounting of things happening in our area. Suppose the same thing happens in another building. Then we know we have a prankster. Suppose it ends here. Then we might begin to suspect something more specific and sinister connected with this building, or with this flat, or with you and your wife as the victims."

"In America . . ."

"This is not America," she said.

She ushered me back into the living room and asked if she could photograph my wounded palms.

"Summing up," she said. "You see your wife in the woods. Then she disappears. There's a face at the window that you think is a dream but is not, because dreams don't leave fingerprints. You run around trying to locate this mysterious figure and injure yourself in the process. Then you pound on the building manager's door and he lets you in, you discover the source of the tape recordings."

"Yes."

"Anything else?" she asked, looking deeply concerned.

I hesitated, not wanting to mention that the face at the window was not entirely Amy's but in fact held the features of the young woman with green hair and the skull bandanna who had been following me in the woods.

"What is it?" the policewoman asked, noticing my distress.

"I can't think of anything," I lied.

She nodded and made another note.

"I think," she said, checking her phone again and turning to leave, "the German word for dream has a similar root to your English word 'trauma.' *Traum*."

"Okay," I said.

"If someone I loved hit me with a block of wood without my permission, I'd be afraid of them."

"Remote entanglement," I said. "Can a person be in two places at once?"

"Not unless they're a witch," she said, lingering in the doorway.

I looked for a sign that she might be joking, but there was no smile or expression indicating anything either way. It was either a German deadpan or else a bald statement of fact.

"Do *you* believe in witches?" I asked.

"Believing is seeing," she said.

"It's the other way around," I said.

"No, it's not," she said. "People see what they want. Call me if you decide to confess."

"To what?"

"Only a little joke," she said. "A test."

"Should I be worried about Rebecca?"

"Not yet," she said. "But please contact me if you plan to leave town."

She flung a business card in my direction, and it sailed perfectly through the air and landed in a corner of the coffee table next to her tea mug. Her name was Veronika.

"Nice," I said.

"You are interesting to my eyes," she said. "I hope that you do not turn out to be a liar. Don't you know that the real meaning of love is equality? It's the dream of a future equality. It's not somebody leaving you all alone in a country where you have no friends or family. It's not somebody beating you up, unless that's your thing, and it's their thing, too, and you agree what's hot before it happens, so that it gets both of you off. You don't know that?"

I winced and turned away so that Veronika couldn't see my reaction. I was about to cry.

"You're very frank," I said.

"The major city here is called Frankfurt," she said. "Call me if anything happens."

I didn't respond.

"I do need you to call me. Especially if you see something in the woods."

"Like what?"

"Just call."

NINE

I waited around for two days without leaving the flat, subsisting on cereal and milk, then just cereal, waiting for something to happen. But Rebecca did not return. There were no more night-fugue episodes with a face at the window. Veronika didn't knock on the door with any news. The building manager didn't drop by. And the recordings of the screaming child had stopped, presumably when the police took the tape machine into evidence.

I couldn't stand it anymore, so I decided to walk down the hill to the station and take the first train to Stuttgart and points north. There was an offer for a day-return fare to Frankfurt displayed on the screen of the ticket machine, so I clicked that and raced to catch the train.

I had not forgotten Veronika's request that I contact her if I left town, but my phone was back at the flat and I didn't have coins for the payphone in the station. Besides, I would be back within the day, and no one would be the wiser. Even if the police came to the flat, I could simply say that I'd missed them because I had been out for a walk.

On the connecting train to Frankfurt from Stuttgart, my reserved seat on the crowded train was facing against the direction of travel, so I popped a motion-sickness pill before the vertigo began its slow spirals towards nausea. But when I awoke, I found myself facing the direction of travel, somehow. I couldn't understand how this was possible, and I didn't recognize the names of the small stations for farm towns that the train was speeding past without stopping.

A ticket collector came by. After I had allayed her initial suspicions that I was trying to ride for free, she took pity on me, waived the penalty fare, and explained what had happened, using hand gestures when her English failed her. The train had docked in Frankfurt and changed directions on its way east. Without moving seats,

I was now headed towards the front. And we were traveling to Berlin, on an intercity express with limited stops.

"What's going on in your country?" she asked me. "Many people in Germany used to look up to America. We became you and you became us?"

"Remote entanglement," I said.

The motion-sickness pills pulled me under again. The next time I woke up I found myself in Ostbahnhof. Leaving the train, I came into the area near the murals adorning the remnants of the Wall that used to separate two mirror cities and two doppelgänger countries. On foot, I followed the river through light rain to the Museum Island, where Nefertiti greeted me in her glass cage, immortal, slim-necked, one eye put out. At the Altes National Museum, a man in his eighties with terrible teeth from the war years stopped me to ask if I happened to be Swedish. He shook his head gloomily when he found out that the answer was Wisconsin (bad), by way of Pilsen (very bad). He kept on insisting in German that I was Swedish, that I could only be Swedish, that there was only one explanation for me and that was my Swedishness.

"You have mistaken me for someone else," I suggested.

"It's Monday," he said, in German.

"And?" I said, in German.

"I'm from Dresden," he said. "It's Monday in Dresden."

"It's Monday everywhere," I said.

"Yes," he said. "But Monday is Monday in Dresden."

Then he added something in German that I didn't understand.

"Sorry?" I said.

"Stay away from Dresden on Monday," he said.

The rain picked up, so I passed quickly by the site of Hitler's Bunker—now a parking lot near the Holocaust Memorial, where children climbed over the concrete maze of larger-than-life stones. I sought cover from the weather in the trees of the Tiergarten, pausing to consider for a moment that I had never been this far east before. Berlin induced a mania for further travel. Why not keep going—Krakow? Warsaw? Budapest? Istanbul? Siberia? Alaska?

I wandered into a grove of trees and found myself confronted with the impossible. Amy had described a tree that looked like a tree but was not a tree. I had blundered into a sculpture of a tree that stood next to a metal installation of table-tennis stands, all empty due to the rain. The table tennis and the tree were made of stainless steel. The tree memorialized something or other.

I must have been sleepwalking again, seeing things. I was actually back in Tübingen, sleeping in our flat. Yes, that must have been it. Or maybe I had never been there, either. Maybe I was sleeping in our house in Vermont, and I had never been to Germany at all. But this was just fatigue and Dramamine talking. My addled brain wasn't clever or imaginative enough to weave together anything so complex as this nested set of dreams. I would have had to invent Germany, so to speak, out of whole cloth, an exhausting process requiring the generation of new cities, an entire language and grammar . . . I had to laugh at myself.

In an instant, I had the feeling that I was being watched. The sense of someone or something tracking my movements from a vantage point in the trees. This and the rain drove me on toward a station near the park, and I gravitated from the S-Bahn system to the main train station. Boarding for somewhere—anywhere, really—seemed easier at this point than finding a room for the night.

On first arriving in Germany, I found the eye contact from the women in the public spaces unnerving. Gradually I recognized these darts and glances for what they were, half-bored curiosity. The Berlin look. Maybe old nightmares had reasserted themselves as lights went out one by one, but for now there was still a secret city to explore and discover. In the parks, the heroin gangs that ruled the parks controlled the refugees who encamped in the crevices of the city, but there were other things to enjoy there, too. Something erotic always hangs in the air of any large train station. The multiplicity of arrivals, flowing exchanges between borders, chance encounters, spying, dead drops, potential assignations. An orgy of anonymity, massed lives shaken and blended together, everyone with or without power trying to get through the day. The signs read Warsaw, Munich, Vienna, Budapest. Young people in traditional costumes, biergarten looks, combined with cyberpunks with pink and purple hair, tourists in Super Mario Brothers getups like the one worn by the employee at the internet cafe, unrelated groups headed to or from fancy-dress events.

Then I saw her again, the hooded figure in the woods, the face at the window, the young woman with glasses and green hair, or someone who looked very much like her, watching me from a bench as I read the ABFAHRTEN/ DEPARTURES display. The resemblance seemed uncanny enough to warrant a closer look. I passed by her, and we exchanged glances. She smiled blandly, nonchalantly, as if I meant nothing to her. But it was the same person, I was almost certain. A metal hook went into my throat, and I found bile backing up into my mouth as I rushed away from her towards a ticket machine.

Within an hour, I found myself on a train to Vienna, then exited the train in Prague and then headed down to

Pilsen, where my mother's family was from. If I could get a postcard stamped there, it would please her to no end. I was thinking that if I saw the green-haired hooded figure again after these changes I could be certain she had followed me. Why had this person stared into my bedroom window at night? I might have mistaken her for Amy as I woke up. It could have been her fingerprints on the glass. I pictured her there, breathing fog on the pane, watching me sleep. Who, why, or how, I had no clue.

I didn't catch sight of her on any of the trains. In Pilsen, some hours later, I wandered into a chain hotel near the station and slept very badly in a room with a chugging air conditioning unit and mosquitoes. In terms of interior design, the room might have been adjacent to a superhighway on the I-95 corridor between Boston and New York City. As I drifted off, I considered that I might in fact be in another place right now. Bilocation, wormholes. My mind unraveled. I needed rest but I woke up around midnight with nothing to do, so I asked at the front desk where to have a drink. Either I had been misunderstood, or there was a particular clientele at this hotel, or the staff were playing a joke on me, or they sent me to the only place that was open at this hour, but the place required a special knock to enter. It was in a basement, with color-coded rooms that were almost entirely empty.

In one of the rooms, an extremely young and good-looking kid, obviously coked to the gills, twirled madly on a sad little metal pole and then started grinding on me.

"*Hallo,*" he said, all tiny white pointed teeth.

"Oh, no," I said. "I'm not German."

"But you smell like the train from Berlin," he said, in English. I couldn't tell if this was a compliment or an accusation. We were completely alone together in a blaring red room.

I didn't want to be rude, so I failed to pull away fast enough when he went for my neck, giving me a playful bite and a quick flick of the tongue. I had to push him back a little, gently, on his shoulder, to signal my lack of enthusiasm, apologizing for myself for reasons that weren't clear to me. I left the place feeling deeply dejected because I was worried that I had misrepresented myself to get in. The night clerk at the hotel asked me with a wide grin if I had enjoyed myself. I gave him two big thumbs up to show that I was a good sport or to refuse to accept that he had outwitted me.

He stopped me in my tracks with an outstretched arm and handed me a postcard, which he said had been hand-delivered while I was out. The note was in block letters in green ink on the back of an image of the Mission Dolores in San Francisco. The postcard read, in Amy's script:

Noon at the bell tower of the tallest church. I'll see you before you see me.

I asked if the person who delivered the note had green hair, and the night clerk frowned.

"Green hair," I said, pointing at my head. "Hair?"

"*Herr?*" he said. "No, a woman."

I held up my hands to my face and curled my fingers around my eyes to resemble fake glasses, and the clerk nodded in confirmation. The clerk raised his eyebrows significantly, but I didn't want to talk to him about it. The woman in the window had followed me all the way here from Tübingen, including the miles on foot across the city of Berlin in the rain and the train change in Prague.

Thinking about Amy's note killed off any possibility of sleeping that night. Alternatives, permutations, time-lines, and stories spun out of my exhaustion, branching paranoias and possibilities. The woman with the green hair couldn't be Amy—she was simply too young. She must have been working for Amy as a messenger. That was the most obvious and simple solution to almost everything that had happened. Unless Amy had aged backwards in her travels, an idea that I didn't wish to consider.

I had some time to kill before the noon appointment on the postcard, so I walked the city where my matrilineal heritage dissipated into the fog of old empires and mass migrations in the nineteenth century. Actually, I didn't know anything about my mother's family except that they were from Pilsen and they didn't like beer. I missed her very much and felt ashamed that it had been so long since our last phone call. I wondered what she would have advised me to do about this meeting in the church tower, an unmissable grand spire smack-dab in the middle of a cobbled square with a planned town center arrayed around it in a rectangle. Small trucks were beginning to arrive for a farmers' market in the square, although the stalls were still under their tarps.

I wandered through the streets to the entrance to the old onion-domed synagogue, which had been one of the largest of its kind in Europe. The building had been used to store the furniture stolen from deported Jews. The congregation had been killed, some two thousand people murdered, with around two hundred survivors, less than half that number living in Pilsen today, according to the placards. Past splendor, war damage, massacre, loss, memory, trauma, Europe. Another museum advertised the liberation of Pilsen by the Americans. Patton's tanks had reached all this way east, beyond Berlin, but to the south, before the deal was cut to relegate Czechoslovakia to the Soviet sphere. When the museum opened, the collection appeared to contain everything from cast-off food ration tins to American magazines, Hershey's bars, film canisters, and movie projectors. The Czechs had saved every scrap, it seemed, hoping to stop time, or reverse it, to give their story an alternate ending.

At breakfast in the shell of a grand hotel with Eastern bloc Cold War fixtures—a "modern" lobby with a retro-futuristic neon chandelier from the 1950s—I tasted the famous local beer from the tap. There was something delirious in the water here or an alchemy in the brewing process that made the beer impossibly refreshing. The restaurant had an unironic Iron Curtain feel about it, suitable for clandestine meetings between spies. This was the right place to meet Amy again, not the church spire, with its faux-*Vertigo* vibes. For a single year hundreds of years ago, I read in some promotional literature with awkward English grammar, Pilsen had been the seat of an empire of some size. The local shops, I noticed, had a quaint habit of using their window displays as little wonder-cabinets, filling up their shelves not just with the consumerist detritus of Amerika but with old-fashioned straight razors, revolvers, broken musical instruments, Soviet-era candy wrappers, and packaging for antique tins of chocolates. It was haphazard and bric-a-brac, pleasingly analogue and not aggressively slick. The present had descended on Pilsen in the form of chain banks, electronics stores, big box hotels, Eurofail development schemes, and groups of stag and hen celebrants from Berlin and London massing for brewery tours at Pilsner Urquell. But the city seemed to have other tricks up its sleeve, sleepy pockets out of which one could conjure curios such as the star chart that graced the clock in the public park outside the row of decaying hotels.

I bought a postcard and wrote a brief "wish you were here" type of message with stars and hearts drawn over it. The obverse held a picture of the city square with the towering church at its center, the place where Amy demanded we meet. I found a shop willing to sell me a stamp and mailed the postcard to my mom. Then I headed to the square itself to meet my fate with Amy, having no idea what to expect, but feeling seasick in Bohemia. Amy and the green-haired woman seemed to know where I was at all times. Their faces merged at my window. The entanglements between this church in Pilsen and the Mission Dolores, from where Amy said she had messaged me from her flat just a couple of days ago. I tried to remember if I had ever told Amy about my mother's heritage in Pilsen, maybe it had come up once or twice. The ending of *Vertigo*, with Scottie witnessing Judy's leap to her death, came into view as I wondered what was about to happen here and now.

Everything crowded together in my mind, with Rebecca's vanishing trick piled on top of these layers of worries. I had been stupid to flee Tübingen (or so it would seem) against the express orders of the police. I should have stayed and searched frantically for my wife. I'd had the intuition, however, that Rebecca wouldn't welcome that. I assumed she had gone away with someone new. And if something more sinister was going on? If she really had disappeared, my actions would appear suspicious. More than that, the police would want to know why I didn't seem to care. It would be difficult to explain the truth. When Rebecca wanted to be left alone, she simply went away for a few days. I always assumed that these holidays were with other lovers, but I never asked her about it. She had always returned in the past, but I knew that one day she wouldn't. She was just a cool-temperature academic type of person. It would have been obnoxious and disrespectful, under normal circumstances, for me to search for her. This was how things stood between us at this point in our marriage. But it wasn't much of an alibi.

As I entered the city square and headed towards the church to confront Amy, I realized a love affair needed three things in order to endure. The first thing was lasting friendship, the second was good sex, and the third was the same view about money. Most relationships failed for the same reason they began—because they provided one or two of these things but not all three. Rebecca had her best sex when she was cheating, and Amy liked to abuse me in bed. These were both friendships that had gotten out of hand. I admired the autonomy and intelligence of both women. Equality's a bitch, but it is better than any of the other alternatives. Hitchcock was wrong about everything. Or, rather, his movies told the truth about how people destroyed themselves, not how life should be lived. Everyone needs love, but not everyone is capable of giving love. That second capacity was the only way out of the spiral. I felt like a dullard who had embraced some cereal-box slogan as my religion. I set myself the goal of becoming a human being. I vowed never to watch another Hitchcock film.

I could have walked away at this point, but I had come a long way, and I wanted to find out if I would see Amy when I walked into that church. I felt a little bit like Kim Novak in the scenes of *Vertigo* when Scottie is dressing her in the suit he wants to see, making her dye her hair blond (again), painting her nails, and fashioning her into his vision of his dead beloved Madeleine. And now I was being dragged toward the church by an invisible arm, not towards love, as I had been dreaming, but towards death, I felt certain. I couldn't help myself.

TEN

The city square featured a Renaissance layout arranged around a Gothic spire. At the entrance of the Cathedral of St. Bartholomew stood a beggar who ranted in Czech and showed me what looked like a disability card or a military discharge badge. When I refused to give him money, he told me that he would call on the Devil.

"I know *Sat*-tan!" he said, in English, implying that I was now under a hex.

"Fantastic," I said, in German. "Send my regards."

My new friend followed me into the church, ranting under his breath in German. Something about death and hell and shit and blood and falling into a hole and being lost. I couldn't tell if he was describing his personal history or predicting my future.

I didn't see Amy in the church. To get away from the spell-casting soothsayer, I followed the signs for the bell tower and began climbing up the stairs. There was a little ticket office or kiosk one flight up where I saw the green-haired girl in the glasses. She was twirling a rack of postcards featuring the building we were standing inside, images of the Cathedral in various seasons, with Czech and English messages printed on the front. Seeing her up close for a sustained look, it was striking how in some ways she resembled a much younger version of Amy and how in other ways she didn't. It was a little bit like when someone's nephew or niece resembles their uncle or aunt more than their parents. There was a sense of time traveling in the mix, a de-ageing effect. She was slightly more rounded than Amy in her features—cheeks, shoulders, and so on—and she stood with her feet arranged in a balletic position.

She had been waiting for me here. When she returned my gaze, then shifted to profile, the resemblance with Amy around the nose and eyes was uncanny. Her slightly upturned upper lip, soft, slightly swollen, pink without lipstick, Amy's most alluring feature, looked almost identical. Clearly she'd been selected—if that was the right word—because of their resemblances. As she turned her back on me and started for the stairs up to the bell tower, I recognized once and for all that this person, not Amy, had been the one standing at my window after midnight, looking in at me sleeping. Her hand at the glass, her fingerprints lifted by the police. I wondered if she had also placed the recordings of the screaming kids in the storage closet next to our bedroom.

I tried to follow her as she bounded up the spiral stone staircase, but the grumpy lady attendant at the little kiosk shouted at me to stop. She was tiny and extremely indignant. I realized that the green-haired woman must have already bought a ticket for the tower, whereas I didn't have one yet. I was losing time and falling behind. This was how the setup worked. I shoved some money—more than was necessary—at the kiosk lady but she gave me a truly hateful look.

"No euros," she said. "This is Czechia."

"How many crowns in a euro? Take it all."

"This is a place of worship, not a *bureau de change*."

"I'm making a donation today," I said. "Love the church. There's like eighteen euros."

"Donation box is over there."

She pointed to a spot near the postcards.

"What's 'Czechia'?" I asked, ignoring her and turning to the stairs, money still on her table.

"Would you call 'France' 'The French Republic'?" she shouted after me. "Use reason!"

I began to trudge upstairs, hearing the echoes of steps several turns of the spiral above me. I had entered a secret and personal cinema experience in which I would recapitulate the critical scene from *Vertigo* in real life. But this recognition also felt deflating and disappointing. The staging was literal, clumsy, duplicative. The staircase was different from the one in the movie—unlike in the film, I wouldn't have to look down through a free-fall drop as I ascended, because these flights were built in spirals rather than rectangles. I'd get my taste of motion sickness when I reached the top of the stairs at the height of the bells overlooking the city square. On the way up, I'd retrace the pattern of the film credits.

I began to feel dizzy as I turned and turned in the narrow spaces as I walked up, gaining altitude and envisioning the movie unfolding in my mind's eye. I had rushed too much at first, and I had to stop to catch my breath and try to shake off the derangement of my inner compass. Surely Amy had arranged all of this for my . . . what would the word be? Entertainment? Suffering? Pleasure? Pain? A wood-block bruise on my brain and heart.

As I climbed higher, I wondered why I wasn't going in the opposite direction. Just leave—this was sound advice from Rebecca-world, the realm of the sensible. Go! That's what Rebecca would do when it was no longer fun. Probably that was what she had done. Fair play to her. Great happiness befall her. Someone should get to experience joy.

Amy would be there, waiting for me at the top of the stairs. Then what? I didn't want to be her doormat anymore, much less a murderee in training.

I started seeing sparkles and dark shapes dancing at the edge of my vision, like in the forest. I looked back to see if anyone was following me, even though I knew the spirals leading down were empty because I would have heard any human footsteps on the stones. These visions were generated by motion-sickness, misfiring neurons in contact with the seashell sounds of my inner ear. Nothing supernatural about any of it, I told myself over and over again, on a loop. As in the film, so too in this theatrical production. No ghosts, hauntings, possessions, or doppelgängers. No spirits from the past inhabiting other bodies. No exchange of souls or transfer of guilt. Just a setup, an abusive game, or maybe a crime. The thought seemed crazy, but I wondered if someone had to die today. That there might be actual physical danger hadn't really sunk in before now. Was Amy planning my death or was she going to kill this green-haired young woman in front of me? Absurd as the idea sounded, I tried to increase my pace, holding onto both sides of the narrowing concrete walls of the staircase with my fingertips as I went up.

As I climbed higher, I began to think about the church tower itself. How would anybody know whether a centuries-old structure built on faith wouldn't fall apart or crumble at any moment. How did the builders know, how could they be certain, or relatively confident, that their work would hold up for hundreds of years? Had there been early blunders and disasters, trial and error? Was some secret knowledge passed down in guilds through the generations of architects and master builders, stone masons and assistants, laborers and apprentices? Why didn't old churches just collapse? Or did they? I envisioned World War II–era American tanks and Russian artillery shaking the town square and this church, rattling walls and weakening structures built with no conception of modern bombs and explosives.

I managed to reach the massive clock in the spire, then the level above it, where the bells waited in silence for the hour of noon. The wind began to whistle through the window shutters, which I was thankful to see remained closed. I made a point of avoiding looking up or down. I knew the area opened into a place where you could fall down several floors and get badly hurt. With the wind picking up, I no longer heard the footsteps of the green-haired person echoing above me, but she must have been up there, because there was nowhere else to go.

When I finally got to the top of the stairs, I was out of breath. Adrenaline and vertigo bombed through my system as I coaxed myself out on the viewing platform overlooking the city, the source of my mother's family DNA. In dream logic, it made sense that when Amy pushed me off, I would merge with her. But Amy wasn't there, just the person that I had followed up the stairs, and who had been following me around for days.

I focused on her face and clung to the side of the platform so that I wouldn't have to look down at the tiny cars, the street market, and the cobbles so many hundreds of feet below. I must have been a pathetic sight. My vision was starting to blur, and the wind brought tears to my eyes.

"Who are you?" I asked her.

Up close, with more sustained attention and intense concentration, I saw, with surprise, that she looked a little bit frightened. This was not what I had pictured. Her green hair flapped wildly in the wind, and she kept pulling it back behind her ears, but it wasn't working. She adjusted her glasses and put an index finger to her lips.

I didn't want to lurch towards her, and in any event I didn't think I could make it beyond the flimsy psychological protection offered by holding on to the edge of the viewing platform.

"Why are you doing this?" I asked.

She again shushed me and looked at her watch.

I took in a glimpse of sky and horizon and felt the terror of falling, but also, for the first time, a small thrill. This is what flight would feel like. This was the bird's view of things. A film from the point of view of a falling camera. The haunted ground would form into a flimsy screen I could pass through easily on the way somewhere else, leaving my broken body behind.

As I slowly adjusted to the situation, I fixed my attention on the green-haired person's intelligent violet eyes, so different from Amy's. It was calming to look at her. I saw notes of concern and puzzlement, maybe even guilt. It was the magic spell of empathy involved in a returned gaze that a stranger might give to someone who had stumbled over on the street. She walked towards me and gave me her hand, firm and cool. Then I saw that the wind had made her tear up, too.

"Sorry," she said, in an English accent. "She promised you would enjoy all of this."

"Amy?"

"M.?"

"That's Amy," I said. "What is this?"

"A memorial service," she said. "You're the only mourner. That's really all I know."

She let go of my hand and looked again at her watch. Then she lifted up four fingers and brought one finger down with each passing second. She ran out of fingers, but nothing happened. She frowned.

"There must be a delay," she said. "I—"

An explosion of ringing bells suddenly cut off her voice, jangling deep in my bones and rippling through my organs. My heart nearly burst, and I wanted to jump just to get away from the immensity of resonating sound waves. But the green-haired person who had been tormenting me now placed her hand on my shoulder and looked intently into my eyes, trying to settle me down. Nothing could be heard between us while the bells pealed, marking the number of hours since the birth of Jesus, the ultimate time traveler. The church accounted for the time the faithful had already waited for the ghost god's return from among the dead. It was 4 am in San Francisco. Dead of morning at the Golden Gate Bridge, where people traveled from across the world to disappear.

She handed me a sealed envelope with my name on it, written in Amy's script using the same green ink as on her postcard. I dully looked at my name and noticed how Amy had written it in sarcastic, looping, ornamental cursive letters. Amy knew that I would never stop thinking about her. The lock on the trap closed forever. I willed myself to focus on my name until my head stopped swimming.

But I was angry and let go of the note, thinking it would fall to the floor. Instead, the wind nabbed it. The envelope floated off over Pilsen, then gradually drifted down like a paper plane, not at all like a plummeting human body, until I lost sight of it in the market stalls below the church. I envisioned Amy stepping from the ledge of a Mission bell tower or diving into San Francisco Bay at Fort Point, where the Pacific roiled below the bridge.

"What happened?" the green-haired person said, after the bells had died down.

"I don't know," I said.

"I didn't read the note, sorry," she said. "Shall we try to find the envelope?"

"I don't know," I said.

This was how Amy and I could be in two places at

once, her here with me, shaking with fear near the top of the church spire, me with her in the green tonic and pickling brine of the violent ocean, picked apart by great whites. I was high up in the wind and simultaneously seasick with Amy's sloshing despair. If she was somewhere laughing, it wasn't from joy.

"What's your name?" I asked my stalker.

"Am I in trouble?" she said. "Could you tell her I delivered the note?"

"I'm not sure if she's around anymore," I said.

I wanted to cry but found I couldn't. I didn't care, I told myself, but that was a lie. If Amy had killed herself, it would haunt me for life. She'd sent me her manuscript as a last gift. My revenge and tiny triumph would be to go on. I asked my young companion if she would mind helping me get to my feet. Her arms were strong. She practically lifted me up and allowed me to lean on her until we were safely back inside the sheltered spiral of the stairwell. Our bodies touched until we reached the level of the bells.

Then we both looked up, startled at the sound of footsteps emerging out of the silence left by the bells. They ascended towards us deliberately, very slowly, and rather loudly. It had to be another tourist, solitary at lunchtime, in search of a view. But I knew better. People have a gait as unique as a fingerprint. Or maybe it was the sound of a certain brand of shoe about which Amy was particular, tapping on stone. I heard a familiar sigh.

The green-haired person seemed to intuit my fear and placed herself between me and the stairs. An impulse to protect a weaker creature. A voice emanated from the gloom at the place where the staircase met the floor of the room of bells. The darkness seemed to multiply and merge, like in a time lapse of growth.

"Wandering." I think that's what the voice said. "This hurts."

Then the darkness shifted and seemed to dissipate, if it had been there at all. The sound of footsteps ceased. I had no urge to follow. We sat together in silence for a few minutes, until the hairs on the back of my arms had settled down a little. The green-haired person tousled my hair like I was a little kid who'd just gotten the wind knocked out of them on the sports field.

"Well, that wasn't part of the plan," she said, feigning cheery bluff Englishness. But her voice sounded keyed up. "Do you think you can walk down now? Because I don't want to stay up here a minute longer."

Once we'd retraced our steps to the ticket office and the postcards, each step accomplished against revolt from every sinew in my body and mind, we found it empty.

My little nest of euros stood ignored on the kiosk lady's table. She was gone. A handwritten sign in Czech stood on the table next to the money, but neither one of us could read whether it said anything more revealing than "Back in Fifteen Minutes." Had the kiosk lady walked up the stairs to tell us something and then seen something that scared her? Maybe she was just having a smoke break down in the market. Had it been some random sightseer who didn't wish to disturb us, or a local victim of suicidal ideation, who turned back as soon as they had a sense that other people were in the bell tower with them? Then why had the sound of the footsteps just vanished? Amy could have paid someone else to play a recording of her voice from her phone. Like the recordings of the children, back in the apartment block, was that what had happened? You could broadcast the recording and then remove your shoes to sneak back down the stairs. The idea felt cheap. Maybe in my heightened state I had mistaken the voice for Amy's or misheard something in Czech as English. But I feared this wasn't true.

"It sounded like her," I said, answering a question no one asked.

"I never heard her voice," she said.

"Did you knock on my bedroom window in the middle of the night?" I asked.

"She said that was your thing."

"Were we . . . supposed to . . . uh . . ."

"She said she would pay me a lot more money if I slept with you."

"Did she tell you I liked to be hit?"

She blushed.

"She said all this would be your dream adventure," she said. "Being stalked."

"How . . ." I started.

"It's all sleight of hand," she said. "Like the postcard message. It doesn't specify this particular church. It just says go to the tallest church in town. They all have bell towers. So the postcard would work in almost any location in Europe. As long as I kept track of you it would work pretty much the same anywhere."

"You got used," I said.

She couldn't look at me any longer.

"You'll be all right," she said. "Can I go?"

I nodded, but she didn't need my permission. While I rested in the kiosk lady's chair, waiting for my blood pressure to dial down, I listened to the young woman's steps get quicker, softer, and more distant. If there had been somebody else on the stairs before, we would have heard them leaving.

Every time I closed my eyes, I saw Amy falling.

Rebecca had left me for another lover.

I waited for Amy's voice, yearning and afraid to hear it again. Such cases were not uncommon. A glimpse of someone recently departed, if that's what had happened. Would I see her again, later, in a shop window or sitting in a passing bus? Now I'd be looking everywhere for her.

When I finally mustered the energy to exit the church, I opened my wallet and gave the Satanist beggar, who remained at his station by the entrance, some spare change. He looked at the money with contempt. Then he told me that my life lay under a curse. He could lift the curse for fifty euros.

I gave him twenty and told him he was too late.

"I pray for you," he said.

"Pray for the Eurozone," I said.

I walked around town, aimlessly and in a state of shock, looking for a good place to cry in the homeland of my mother's people, this place of botched liberation and failed empires, perennially occupied territory, the Kafkaland taps from which the world's supply of good beer flowed, a landlocked country in the seas of Bohemia where people greeted one another by saying something like sailors, "Ahoy." It was time to get drunk and see if I could find someone in Pilsen who wanted to hurt me. That shouldn't be difficult to find.

ELEVEN

I boarded a Czech Railways "Alex" train bound for Munich, changed again in Stuttgart, and arrived back at our flat in Tübingen after midnight. The first train was a bone-rattling Cold War–era charmer with vinyl bench seats and windows in the corridor that could lower to decapitation level if you leaned your head outside at the wrong moment. A comically large steel lever near the window was illustrated to indicate red for heat and blue for air conditioning. When I turned it, something in the walls whirred uselessly, producing no cool air. I felt affection

for the older women conductors, in their smoked glasses
and their clean, faded uniforms and meticulous caps, the
Czech coffee kid with his cart, the clumsy thick coins and
large-denomination bills, the deflated Eastern European
prices in crowns, the whole apparatus of charming Bo-
hemian dedication to constant failure from which my
mother's family had fled, only to break on the rocks of
the Midwest. There was a story told in the bars of Pilsen
about how the Soviet commissars had demanded that
the famous brewery modernize by replacing its copper
pipes with stainless steel. Clearly this was some scheme
to make work in the forges of the USSR and not good for
the taste of the hops and water. The brewmasters had ignored the orders from Moscow—some things, like beer,
were more important than life. Pilsner had lived for another generation before becoming subsumed in the shiny
shell world of global Amerika.

On this old slow train open to the outside air, I never
once felt motion sickness.

Thinking about anything other than Amy's proba-
ble suicide seemed like a good idea, but it was the pro-
verbial polar bear that appeared whenever I told myself
not to think about it. In her own mind, Amy was Gavin
Elster, I thought, the puppeteer murderer in *Vertigo* who

enlists Judy Barton to help kill his wife Madeleine and drive Scottie insane as the impotent witness to her death, like me. So Amy was both Elster and Madeleine, the murderer and the victim. Or perhaps she was becoming Carlotta, now, the ghost. A phrase from *Vertigo* repeated itself in my mind. It was about men in the old days mistreating women: *They had the power and the freedom*. But that had always been Amy. She had reversed the clock so that time ran backwards or stood still. Some part of me stood forever on the ledge of the spire. Amy would never allow death to be something inflicted on her. She passed through the haunted screen and now she could go wherever she liked.

In Munich, I knew, we had passed near Dachau, and the train lines that followed the spiderwebs of tracks to the destinations of former subcamps where, within living memory, prisoners had been worked and starved to death in the plains and foothills of Bavaria and the resort mountains of the Tyrol. I had studied a map of these subcamps in a museum. I was accustomed to the pictures of large-scale death factories and vast nightmare prisons from documentaries, but it was the sheer number and geographical spread of the smaller subcamps that I could not shake. Back home they fought over statues of Confederate generals in public squares, while the plantations transformed themselves into wedding venues.

Rebecca had found herself in Germany surrounded by intelligent colleagues who desired her otherness as Mrs. Danvers had another Rebecca's in the Hitchcock film, rubbing herself with Rebecca's furs at Manderley. Or maybe that was me. I needed a Rebecca, but I had chosen a Rebecca who wasn't a Rebecca. My wife lacked the requisite cruelty. Amy was my Rebecca, and both of them had killed themselves in order to live on forever as a specter in the west wing. These thoughts felt tainted, ugly. In truth Rebecca and I had never had anything more than a friendship. She was a cool star, and we'd never had that intense love that everyone deserves but not everyone gets. After what had happened in the tower in Pilsen, I was ready for Rebecca to divorce me, and I wished my wife all the fun in the world. She could have our house in Vermont. I'd travel back to Prague and points east with my buyout money. I would join the world's growing ranks of useless men. I would try to arrange for Amy's manuscript to find a publisher, so that her final book would see the light of day under her own name. Amy was copper and I was stainless steel—like the brewmasters at Pilsner Urquell, I wouldn't alter the recipe. I wouldn't edit the book except for errors or work on straightening its crooked lines or finding a perfect gray suit in which to dress it up into serious scholarship when it was, in fact, a cri de cœur. I wouldn't do her nails or try to put her hair up, like an undertaker. That wouldn't be the right way to put her ghost to rest.

On arrival, I found Rebecca packing her things at the flat.

"Oh," she said, when she saw that I'd caught her leaving me.

"Hi," I said.

"I won't apologize," she said. "That would be disingenuous. I'm not sorry."

"Listen," I said. "Amy killed herself. At least I think she did."

"Now I am sorry," Rebecca said. "But I'm still leaving."

"I know."

"There's someone."

"I know."

"Damn it, I am so sorry."

Rebecca advanced toward me, stood on her tiptoes, said my name, and gave me a goodbye hug. It wasn't intended to be a condescending gesture; it was just something by which she wanted to remember me.

"Try to enjoy your life sometimes," she said from the

open doorway, with her little roller suitcase standing between us. "It's the only one you've got. And try some anti-depressants? They work."

"We should have been friends," I said. "But now we'll never be friends."

"Yes," she said.

"You're doing the right thing," I said.

"Thanks for saying that," Rebecca said.

"This hurts," I said.

"Would it help to have sex?" she said.

"No," I said.

"Want to try it anyway?" she said.

I was ashamed of being unable to say no, but we had to stop when I started crying.

The next afternoon, I awoke to someone knocking, firmly and insistently, at the door to our flat. It was the police-woman, Veronika. She'd dyed her hair purple, with pink streaks at the fringes framing her face. She looked at me with a mixture of genuine curiosity and what felt like slight suspicion. She was wearing glasses today, and she wore plain clothes, high-waisted gray wool trousers, a green velour blazer, and a brightly colored scarf that re-capitulated the shades of the blazer and her black men's dress shirt. She wore sturdy walking shoes and had a small leather backpack looped around one shoulder.

"Come with me," she said.

I couldn't figure out what was going on at first. We walked in silence to the door of the building manager, who she also disturbed with her incessant knocking.

"What is it?" the manager asked, in German, tipping his Tirolean cap to the officer.

"Why did you place recordings of screaming children in the room next to this man's flat?" she asked him, deadpan, in English, so that I could follow along.

Rather than denying it, he gulped.

"Well?" she pressed him.

"I hate Americans," he said, in German.

"Why?" she said.

"Look at everything they're doing," he said, in English.

"That's all?" Veronika asked, in English.

"I wanted him to leave," he said.

"Where did the recordings come from?" she asked.

"Movies," he said, in English, then added another word, in German.

"He said horror movies," Veronika translated for me, but I already knew the word.

"Many children scream in horror movies," he explained to both of us, in English.

"Would you like to have him charged?" she asked me, without taking her eyes off him.

"Not really," I said. "For what?"

The building manager closed his door on us, abruptly. Veronika turned to me.

"We solved a mystery!" she said.

"How did you know it was him?" I asked.

"I didn't," Veronika said, smirking, dimples appearing on her freckled cheeks below her sleepless-looking eyes.

"Just a guess?" I said.

"Process of elimination," she said. "He knows the building. Only a few people would have any reason to be in that room. Now we must talk about *you*. Let's walk into the forest."

"Did you ever find a match for the fingerprints on my window?" I asked.

"Should I try?" she asked. "Rain might have washed them away from the glass. I suppose the images are still on my phone, but I'm not sure it's worth all the trouble and expense."

"You're right," I said.

We followed the paved little road that ran along the ridge past the allotments and the "MDEAD" graffiti next to the inverted cross on the electrical box. I wondered if the tag was just a coincidence, or if the green-haired girl had been instructed by Amy to paint it. It didn't matter anymore.

We wandered deeper into the woods, along a footpath strewn with pine needles. Everything looked slightly different than it had before, slightly sharper, more welcoming, and less alien. The forest was just a forest again. I felt I was seeing it for the first time.

"We found your wife," Veronika said. "It was as you expected. She was with a work colleague in a resort near the Swiss border. Very embarrassing for all concerned."

"I spoke with her last night," I said. "She dropped by to collect her suitcase."

"I must ask you something," she said. "Why did you leave town? I specifically asked you not to do that."

"I left the country," I said. "Sort of by accident."

I explained a little bit about my journey, how I had intended to take a day trip to Frankfurt and had wound up on a train to Berlin instead, and then decided to visit Pilsen because it was the place where my mother's ancestors had lived.

"Pilsen?" Veronika said. "Did you tour the brewery? It's very good."

"Not exactly," I said.

I thought it might be better to leave out Amy's story for now. Too long-winded and confusing. And about the green-haired girl from Britain who had followed me and left her fingerprints on Veronika's camera images. Even if they could locate her, there was no reason to land her in trouble with the German police. We didn't have to talk about it today. It was a nice feeling, knowing that.

The sun tracked our progress through the oaks, pines, and birches, falling intermittently into moody patches of shadows and pools of cool darkness. Fresh air and little pockets of mist radiated through the branches, as if the trees were breathing alongside us. I noticed that the paths were mostly deserted.

"More rain predicted," Veronika said.

"Are you at work right now?" I asked.

"No," she said, giving me a sidelong look. "Listen, I should tell you something. I'm leaving the police force. It's just not for me."

We took yet another branching subpath and began to descend into the valley where the trail led down to Bebenhausen and the ancient monastery. Veronika took my hand.

"Is this all right with you?" she said.

She squeezed my hand.

"*You're* Scottie," I said. "Not me. I just realized."

"What?" Veronika said, laughing.

"You've never seen *Vertigo*?" I asked.

"Alfred Hitchcock?" she said. "Not for ages. For a soon-to-be-ex-police officer this film is a little bit silly. In terms of its portrayal of modern procedures. I never thought you had done anything really horrible, by the way. But one must exhaust all plausible alternatives."

We walked another few miles, past Bebenhausen and deeper into the forest, following a trail where I had never been before. A gliding hawk guided us to a shelter at the top of a gentle hill. The sun was starting to fade into massing clouds that looked like they might presage a downpour, but neither one of us wanted to return to the town. We'd been walking for hours, I realized from the position of the sun, but it had seemed like we had just started talking. Bursts of wild sunlight suffused the woods in glory, preliminaries to the storm. We passed through what looked like the calmest place in the world, in a region of a country where absolute evil had once prevailed and then had receded or had been bombed deep underground. The contradictions were impossible and yet the country had survived and lived with itself somehow and not died and had not forgotten but instead found ways to grow back and could always tip back into the abyss. Obviously I didn't know anything about Germany. This century was shaping up to be yet another shitstorm, here as everywhere, but, at least for this afternoon, none of that

mattered. Veronika's gift to me was to experience this forest without fear.

We sat on a small bench inside the little shelter, side by
side rather than across from one another.

"It's going to rain," I said. "Do you have an umbrella
in that bag?"

"Hmmm," she said. "Let's take a look."

She set the backpack on the small table in front of us.
Out rolled beer bottles and a can of black spray paint
wrapped in a bright red bandanna.

"Oh," she said, "I forgot the bottle opener."

She pulled the caps off with her teeth and handed me
a sweaty, cool Paulaner to clink against hers. She told me
a little bit about herself. University, a dislike of intellec-
tuals, a desire to return to her hometown and to join a
helping profession, pride in her job tainted by the usual
bullshit, annoying colleagues, and a recent, burning pas-
sion for English spy novels set in Germany. I soaked it
in. I wanted to listen to Veronika talk all day and into
the evening. I wanted to tell her everything that had
happened.

She untied the bandanna from the can of spray paint
and then wound it around her nose and mouth. She took
up the spray paint and began marking the concrete wall
inside the shelter as the first raindrops fell through the
leaves above us.

She made what at first looked like an *x*, but it was slightly tilted on its axis. Then she turned it into an inverted cross.

"Now you know my secret," she said.

"You said you're into the sick shit?" I asked.

Veronika blushed, but not happily.

"It's a perfectly healthy expression of, well," she said. "You really need to let go of these puritanical Americanisms holding you back from the full range of, you know. Oh, you're joking."

"I'm just nervous," I said. "Actually, I was hoping to learn more."

She checked to see that I was in earnest.

"Any time," she said. "I have a pamphlet."

"How old are you?" I said, laughing.

"Forty-seven," she said. "Life's most depressing year. According to science."

I watched her as she undid the bandanna and looked over her handiwork somewhat skeptically. There was a slight shake or swerve at the top of the inverted cross.

"What does this mean?" I asked.

"Black metal," she said. "Like I said, I'm into the sick shit. I'm kind of a witch. Would you like to be friends?"

"Just friends?" I asked.

"You would look pretty in a collar but you're not ready for me," she said.

"Oh," I said. "I thought . . ."

"I know what you thought," she said. "You're tender."

It was a strange word to use. Maybe something vital was lost in translation.

"What should we talk about?" I asked.

"Just watch," she said.

"What?"

"You have to concentrate, or you'll miss it."

Veronika pointed into the gloaming beyond the hill, where shadows gathered in the trees and lightning sprang from the horizon, jutting from the bruised distance where we could sense the foothills receding far away into the Alps, the crackling and booming of the storm closing in.

"Conditions must be correct," she said. "Even then it's not certain to appear. Ah, there."

Something happened. Some of the shadows at the edge of our vision merged and darkened until they appeared larger than normal. Then an oval shape developed like an image in a photographic darkroom. The shape grew even larger in size and then lost its oval outline, seeping into a more oblong form about the height of a very tall person as it drifted across the forest at nightfall, obscuring the view of the surrounding trees and shrubs. It was less like a mirror or a portal or a screen than the entrance to a darkened room that had its door removed from its hinges. If I turned my eye directly towards the shape, it became less visible, as if it operated on different principles of inhabiting space than the rest of the world surrounding it.

"That's . . ." I whispered. It was a question.

"I don't know," Veronika said. "You can talk. Sound doesn't seem to bother them."

Veronika's use of the plural startled me. I already knew that Amy had been half-right all along, but maybe there was more than one of these shapes rattling around the globe, or maybe each encounter was a different experience for each person.

"I think I saw this before," I said.

The shape paused and then, for lack of a better word, it beckoned. Nothing could be seen inside it, but I couldn't avoid the sense that it contained something that I needed. It emanated a certain smell, like a chemical process, not unpleasant, almost like Midwestern American lilacs late in summer that were slightly overripe. I found this oddly comforting at first, but then I wondered if the shape could somehow tap into my memories and alter my sense perceptions. Maybe that smell was just for me. The dark shape shimmered very slightly, almost dancing with constellations of silvery light as it expanded again into a more squarelike formation. The shape seemed sentient as it morphed into academy ratio. The signals, if that's what the lights were, went dark again, blinking out.

"Does it . . . ?" I said. "Can we?"

"Go in?" Veronika said. "I've never tried."

"Did you?" I said.

"Conjure it?" she said. "No. At least I don't think so. I've seen it a few times before. Just before a thunderstorm. I think maybe it . . . *likes* me?"

"Do you think it takes you somewhere else?"

"Maybe," she said. "Yes, I get that feeling."

I thought about what might happen if we went inside the shape. Would I see San Francisco Bay? Would ghostly Amy be there? Or another Veronika? Maybe I'd see myself in some other timeline. Would time move backwards? I got the feeling that I wouldn't be able to return from wherever it led. Maybe that wouldn't be so bad. But I wasn't ready to leave.

"Is it like a black hole?"

"Do you want to go in?" Veronika said. "Together?"

"I'm afraid," I said, without hesitation.

"I know," she said. "I've thought about disappearing. I think it knows that. I think they know that about us and seek us out. I think they're very old. I think they live in the caves around here."

"I'd like to stay here, with you," I said. "If that's okay."

"I needed someone else to see it," she said. "Not just anyone."

She held my hand again and gave it a jolly, playful

shake. When I looked up from our interlaced fingers to Veronika's face, she wasn't looking at me anymore. She was watching the place where the dark shape had been, with an almost grief-stricken expression. I followed her gaze across the dimming forest, but the shape had vanished. Everything felt full, as if a certain kind of energy had transferred itself to the wind in the trees. A sense of relief rushed in. The intervals between lightning and thunder were getting shorter, seven seconds, then four. The sharp smell of ozone overwhelmed me. I looked forward to sharing a pot of tea with Veronika after our good drenching, after everything, finally, poured down from the sky.

ACKNOWLEDGMENTS

My extraordinary editor, Jill Meyers, offered incisive comments and brilliant support throughout my creative process. Endless thanks to Will Evans and the team at Deep Vellum. My colleague, Anne Chapman, helped me see one key element that was missing from my story. Gratitude for feedback on early drafts goes to Brian Baker, David Gassaway, Jim Gavin, Michael McGriff, Emily Mitchell, Dan O'Brien, Joseph Pearson, and Suzanne Rivecca. While Alfred Hitchcock's *Vertigo* (1958) is referenced throughout, in truth I drew as much from *Rebecca* (1940). This book is dedicated to Lotte Eisner.

ABOUT THE AUTHOR

J. M. Tyree is the editor of *Film Quarterly* and the coauthor (with Michael McGriff) of *Our Secret Life in the Movies*, an NPR Best Books selection. A former Capote-Stegner Fellow in Fiction at Stanford, he has published in *American Short Fiction, Brick, McSweeney's, New England Review, Sight & Sound*, and in the BFI Film Classics series of books on film from Bloomsbury and the British Film Institute. He is an associate professor in the Cinema Program at VCUarts.

ABOUT A STRANGE OBJECT

Founded in 2012 in Austin, Texas, A Strange Object champions debuts, daring writing, and striking design across all platforms. The press became part of Deep Vellum in 2019, where it carries on its editorial vision via its eponymous imprint. A Strange Object's titles are distributed by Consortium.